"Mom Usually Doesn't Sleep This Late,"

Sybil's daughter Emily told Duncan while she played with her kitten on the kitchen floor. "She must be really tired."

Duncan knew exactly why Sybil was so tired. Luckily, his brother had brought Emily back home from her slumber party *after* he'd left her mom's bedroom.

"The least you could do is button your shirt straight and put on your boots, Duncan," his brother whispered with humor in his voice.

Suddenly, Emily glanced at Duncan and studied his morning stubble. She watched him slowly rebutton his shirt and pull on his boots. There was nothing light in his feelings for her mother, and he knew Emily understood that.

Very carefully the girl said, "I like to wear just my socks when I'm at home, too, Duncan."

Dear Reader,

It's hard to believe that this is the grand finale of CELEBRATION 1000! But all good things must come to an end. Not that there aren't more wonderful things in store for you next month, too....

But as for June, first we have an absolutely sizzling MAN OF THE MONTH from Ann Major called *The Accidental Bodyguard*.

Are you a fan of HAWK'S WAY? If so, don't miss the latest "Hawk's" story, *The Temporary Groom* by Joan Johnston. Check out the family tree on page six and see if you recognize all the members of the Whitelaw family.

And with *The Cowboy and the Cradle* Cait London has begun a fabulous new western series—THE TALLCHIEFS. (P.S. The next Tallchief is all set for September!)

Many of you have written to say how much you love Elizabeth Bevarly's books. Her latest, *Father of the Brood*, book #2 in the FROM HERE TO PATERNITY series, simply shouldn't be missed.

This month is completed with Karen Leabo's *The Prodigal Groom,* the latest in our WEDDING NIGHT series, and don't miss a wonderful star of tomorrow— DEBUT AUTHOR Eileen Wilks, who's written *The Loner and the Lady*.

As for next month...we have a not-to-be-missed MAN OF THE MONTH by Anne McAllister, and Dixie Browning launches DADDY KNOWS LAST, a new Silhouette continuity series beginning in Desire.

Lucia Macro

Senior Editor

Please address questions and book requests to:
Silhouette Reader Service
U.S.: 3010 Walden Ave., P.O. Box 1325, Buffalo, NY 14269
Canadian: P.O. Box 609, Fort Erie, Ont. L2A 5X3

CAIT
LONDON
THE COWBOY AND
THE CRADLE

SILHOUETTE *Desire*

Published by Silhouette Books

America's Publisher of Contemporary Romance

To Isabel, Lucia and my special editor, Melissa Senate.

SILHOUETTE BOOKS

ISBN 0-373-76006-X

THE COWBOY AND THE CRADLE

CAIT LONDON

lives in the Missouri Ozarks but loves to travel the Northwest's gold rush/cattle drive trails every summer. She loves research trips, meeting people and going to Native American dances. Ms. London is an avid reader who loves to paint, play with computers and grow herbs (particularly scented geraniums right now). She's a national bestselling and award-winning author, and she also writes historical romances under another pseudonym. Three is her lucky number; she has three daughters, and the events in her life have always been in threes. "I love writing for Silhouette," she says. "One of the best perks about all this hard work is the thrilling reader response and the warm, snug sense that I have given readers an enjoyable, entertaining gift."

Dear Reader,

I'm thrilled to be participating in Desire's CELEBRATION 1000. It's the perfect time to introduce The Tallchiefs of Amen Flats, Wyoming. As a writer who loves cowboys and strong Western women, I've been waiting to tell their stories. Descended from a Scottish bondwoman and the Sioux chieftain who captured her, the Tallchief family is proud and not easily tamed by love.

Orphaned in their teens, five Tallchiefs struggle to stay together and keep their ranch on Tallchief Mountain. They unite to return their great-great-grandmother's dowry to the Tallchief family. Each piece bears a legend with it, which concerns love. (I also love legends and heritages.) Duncan, the eldest, is to find the Tallchief cradle.

The ultimate and untamed cowboy, he is a loner and leads the Tallchiefs' legends with "...a woman who brings the cradle to a man of Fearghus blood and fills it with his babies."

I invite you to share in the legends and loves of the Tallchiefs, beginning with *The Cowboy and the Cradle*, part of Desire's CELEBRATION 1000.

Cait London

*The woman who brings the cradle
to a man of Fearghus blood
will fill it with his babies.*

Prologue

———

"**W**ipe your nose, Fiona," eighteen-year-old Duncan, the eldest Tallchief, told his ten-year-old sister. October layered fire-colored leaves over the graves of their parents, buried that day on Tallchief Mountain. "Nothing is going to separate us. We'll be just the same, only Mom and Dad won't be here."

Duncan fought the pain inside him. And the guilt. The day their parents were murdered, he'd argued bitterly with his father.

"I'm scared," Fiona stated, clutching Duncan closer, her long legs dangling down him as he held her on his hip. "Why did that bad man have to shoot Mom and Dad?"

Duncan adjusted the blanket around her, the one she had been fighting and crying into during her nightmares. Inexperienced in taking the place of his comforting, calm mother, he'd swept Fiona up in his arms, shielding her from the storm's mist and the night. He'd taken her to his special place overlooking the lake. He'd done his share of crying apart from the rest, not wanting them to see him in pain and fear. Could he hold them together? Could he protect the four younger ones?

Duncan straightened his shoulders. He would do his best and better.

Wyoming's cold autumn winds whipped around Tallchief Mountain, sweeping through Duncan's mourning heart. The wind lashed whitecaps on the small, icy lake. The jutting rocks and lush meadows had reminded their great-great-grandmother, Una Fearghus, of her home in Scotland.

When the convenience-store robbery occurred, two customers had just dropped in. Pauline and Matt Tallchief had decided to bring their hungry brood home a treat: enormous pizzas with every topping possible. They had been traveling, buying a new, long-horned hairy sheep. The Scottish ram was for their small herd; cattle and wild, proud children were the Tallchiefs' main crops.

Now they were gone, and Duncan held his frightened baby sister. Calum, the second eldest at seventeen, swooped out from behind a pine branch and glared at Duncan through the night. "So you've got her. You should have left a note."

Then Birk, the third son, pushed through the bushes, wrapped in his quilt. He glared at Elspeth, who was just behind him. "See? I told you Duncan would take care of her. Stop nagging."

Duncan held Fiona closer; he'd known his brothers would find them. Matthew Tallchief had been a top tracker, equaled by few in his lifetime. His sons and daughters were almost as skilled.

Duncan rocked his sister, needing her against him for comfort as much as she needed him. Calum, Birk and Elspeth moved as one, keeping very close in the storm.

The three brothers had immediately taken to the mountain after the killer; Elspeth had taken care of Fiona. When they returned, three sets of gray, determined eyes had leveled at the sheriff. "Here's your man. No one is separating us," Duncan had stated flatly.

"We're staying together," Calum had added in his too-soft, precise tone.

"On Tallchief Mountain." Birk, usually laughing and boisterous, had nodded curtly. He looked as grim and determined as the other two Tallchiefs.

They had tracked the killer throughout the night, going places the sheriff would not have taken his men until full light. At dawn, while the sheriff's men were still checking their riding gear, the three grim Tallchief sons had ridden into Amen Flats, the killer in tow, made to walk every step. They'd left their boyhoods behind.

When the sheriff had heard the Tallchief clan was on the killer's trail, he'd deliberately dragged his feet. No one could track in the night like the Tallchiefs, and once they set their minds to a task they did it. They were bred from a Sioux chieftain who had once hunted the lawless.

Duncan pushed away his grief. He had a big job in front of him. He had to unite his family so that no one could tear them apart. The Tallchiefs were born to challenges. He turned to his brothers and sisters, raising his right hand. "Hold up your thumbs."

"Aye, sir!" The Tallchiefs immediately obeyed his command, right thumbs shoved skyward.

"See that scar? The tiny one that Mom blistered our backsides for cutting. We've sworn to hold one another safe, and we will. Do you swear it?"

"Aye!" The Tallchief cry carried in the wind, sailing over the rocky mountain and the white crests of the deep waves.

"No one is separating us. We'll live here just as before. Calum?"

"Aye, Duncan the defender." Calum stepped up to Duncan and waited for his orders. As children they'd followed Duncan into scrapes and perilous adventures, shouting the Scottish "Aye!" But this was more than skinny-dipping in the icy lake, or waylaying bullies, or stealing their mother's freshly baked pies cooling on the windowsill, or finding a renegade bear and calling him out. Calum recognized what Duncan meant to do, to reassure his family on scant crumbs.

"Calum the cool." Duncan used their childhood names. Heritage ran deep in the Tallchiefs, their blood a blend of a Scottish bondwoman and the Sioux chieftain who had captured her. "You are now in full charge of accounts and payments. Check with the vet to see if there was anything Dad was planning to do with the cattle that we didn't know about.

Check the hay baler and machinery and see what is owed. Do your damnedest.''

He shot a look at Elspeth, who was just parting her lips. At fourteen, Elspeth disdained almost everything about her brothers. According to her, they were savages with endlessly empty bellies. She and Calum possessed the calm genes of the Tallchiefs. Elspeth had a quiet strength and nurturing that would be tested. He ached for her and the burden she would carry. "I know. I am disgusting and crude and you love me. I'll watch the swaggering, the bullying and the bad language.... Elspeth the elegant, you list what needs to be done in the house. We're 'reconfiguring' as Calum says. From now on, no one leaves a dirty dish or tosses their clothes everywhere. Clean out the bathroom when you're done, etc., etc. Or Elspeth will have your backside scrubbing floors. Mine, too. Got it?''

"Aye," she said, crossing her arms.

Like Fiona, she wore long, black braids. But for the gray of her eyes, she could have been an Indian princess. When it came to a good fight, Elspeth would be inventive. "I will and the pigs will be punished. Duncan, I'd love to see you scrub a floor, so watch it.''

"You make lists, Elspeth. We'll all help. Birk the rogue?'' Duncan looked at the third eldest Tallchief.

"Correction. That's Birk the beloved," he returned, preening a bit in the night and lifting an arm to flex and study. "Girls like me.''

"Lacey MacCandliss doesn't. She hates your guts. You're disgusting," Elspeth shot back.

"And me?" Fiona asked Duncan, brushing the tears from her eyes.

The pain in her tone matched the pain he felt, but he would never show it.

"What about me, Duncan? What do I do?''

His eyes softened when he looked at her, this last child of his parents. "Why, Fiona the fiery, you make us happy. You mind your grades and always remember to call me your king.''

Duncan touched her nose with his finger, a gesture she knew meant he was very serious.

"No more fights on the school ground for causes that aren't yours. No more pranks. We're walking a tight line, Fiona. Do you understand?"

She nodded sheepishly and fluttered her lashes. "I will be Miss Goody Two-Shoes, my king."

Duncan didn't believe her innocent look, but he knew she'd try. Her siblings hooted, then Fiona threw Duncan a punch of her own. "Will you sleep next to me tonight, Duncan?"

He didn't hesitate. "Aye. I'll always be here when you need me."

"Me, too," Calum stated loudly, straightening.

"Me, three," Birk shouted to the cold October wind.

Elspeth jabbed him lightly in the arm. She cuddled close to Fiona. "Fiona, I'll sleep with you every night," she whispered. "Duncan, are we really safe?"

"We'll put some glue in it, as Dad used to say. We'll make it." He was scrambling now, fighting the realistic fear that the children's agencies would come calling...or perhaps the bank. They'd have a hard fight of it. He reached into the storm and latched on to a bit of glue—a whimsical murmuring of his mother swirled around him. He ached and mourned for a heartbeat, then stepped into the role he must play to keep the family safe. "In Una's journals she mentions her dowry, which was sold to keep Tallchief Mountain. I think..."

He glanced into the shadows, and found his brothers and sisters leaning forward, latching on to what he said. A tall, rawboned clan, they had the same raven hair as their Sioux great-great-grandfather and the steady, gray eyes of their Scottish great-great-grandmother. They were a tough brood, all rugged angles and tempers and stubborn, bred from Wyoming stock. They'd need that steel to get through this one. "I think that each of us should pledge to return Una's dowry to the Tallchief family. We can do it if we try." *Could they keep together? Could they?*

"Aye! To Una's dowry!" the Tallchief siblings yelled, strong together.

Calum, always sensible, quietly asked, "What about college for you, Duncan? You were to start in January. If Dad hadn't had heart trouble, you would have already been gone."

"You'll go, when the time comes. And the rest of you. I'd rather be here with my family, but I'll work on my education. Dad and Mom are going to be proud of each one of us," Duncan said, quieting the fears of the others.

At eighteen, and with the support of good family friends, Duncan just might pull off the difficult task of keeping his family together. "Each of you better bring home A's and mind your P's and Q's, because we'll pay hard if you don't. Now, lift your thumbs and swear that you'll do your best to try... just try."

The Tallchiefs shot their thumbs high into the stormy sky and cried in unison, "Aye! We are the Tallchiefs and we will make it through!"

One

Duncan Tallchief uncoiled his six-foot-four-inch, lean body from the bar at Maddy's Hot Spot. Shielded interest flickered in Birk's and Calum's expressions, as they sat, feet propped up on the tavern's scarred table.

Jack Smith, belligerent and drunk, had just come calling for Duncan...with four of his drinking buddies. With reddened eyes Jack glared at the man keeping him from his battered wife. Jack, a powerful bricklayer, needed his wife at home. He knew how to deal with a complaining, runaway wife. The one man barring him from Wyonna stood with deceptive ease, a tough breed of Wyoming cowboy who drew women's eyes by just walking. The Tallchief men were all like that, Jack thought. But Duncan protected Jack's wife, and the bully's pride had been cut. "I want my wife," Jack demanded again. "It's time she came home."

This time Jack planned to bog her down with brats; then she'd stay put.

Duncan's gray eyes flashed. "Wyonna has finally realized she's not to blame for your hard times. She's made her choice."

Maddy, the bartender, glanced uneasily at his new mirror sprawling behind the bar. A veteran of the tavern business, he knew that a night like this could brew a brawl.

October made the Tallchiefs restless, stirred their emotions. Years ago on this day they had buried their parents and fought the world to stay together. The bartender eyed Jack Smith. The man was a fool to seek out the Tallchiefs on a night like this.

Especially Duncan. Packed with muscle from ranch work, he was heavier and more broadly built than his brothers. While he looked too solid to move quickly, Maddy had seen Duncan easily vault over a rodeo fence to save a little girl. Maddy pushed his cigar to the other side of his mouth, chewing it. Duncan was a hard man who set his own rules.

Liquor and four of his buddies gave Jack Smith the backbone he needed to walk into the tavern, calling out Duncan Tallchief. "You've messed in my life for the last time, Tallchief," Jack sneered as Duncan faced him.

Duncan's careless stance belied the anger Jack had pricked. He slowly drew on the leather working gloves tucked into his belt, pushing aside the need to color Jack's face the way Wyonna's had been, swollen and bruised, three days ago. He'd found her huddled in a battered pickup near his ranch, and now she was safe.

It was then that Duncan had decided what to do with the small house he owned in town. Lucky, an old cowpuncher, had willed his house to Duncan for good use. Women and children needed protection from men like Jack; the house would do nicely.

Duncan's isolated, mountain "castle," the remodeled Tallchief house, wasn't the place for Wyonna; she needed a woman's care and no gossip. Lacey MacCandliss had tucked Wyonna safely under her wing. A sane man would think twice before facing Lacey over an issue of abuse.

"Let it go, Jack. You're drunk."

"I'm in the mood for a good one, Duncan," Birk offered easily.

Calum tipped his chair back against the wall, glanced at the picture of a nearly naked woman above him and braced his beer on his flat stomach. "There's only five of them. Hardly enough to break Duncan's sweat."

"I think Jack and I can settle this without your help," Duncan drawled in a tone more commonly used for discussing the weather.

Maddy glanced uneasily at the brothers, aware of them sizing up Jack and his gang. "Mind the mirror," he muttered, and dialed Elspeth for help.

Duncan shot Maddy a disgusted glance, his hard jaw contracting. The tavern owner kept Elspeth's number near the phone; Duncan recognized Maddy's frown and said, "Elspeth will spoil the fun."

"I'll teach you a lesson, Tallchief. You tell me where my woman is." Jack threw a punch that Duncan easily sidestepped.

Duncan smiled coolly, showing a row of white teeth against dark skin covered with black stubble. The wind whipped through the open door, catching his longish black hair and lifting it away from his face. Whoever had entered the tavern didn't distract Jack from his next punch. It slashed through the air near Duncan's cheek. The five men were upon Duncan like a pack of wolves.

Sybil stood in the shadows near the tavern door. The large, wood-lined room, studded with pictures of cattle drives and nearly naked women, exploded in the sound of grunts, labored breathing and body slams. She breathed quietly, furious with the man who was outnumbered and clearly enjoying the brawl.

Music for a fast-moving two-step slid from the jukebox, background music for primitive male grunts.

Duncan—she recognized the jutting angles of his face and the slashing, black brows—grinned almost boyishly as he ducked a punch. The grin died, replaced by a dark anger, as another punch connected against his flat stomach. He had the ruthless, cold look of Satan about him then, not fitting his code name "Mother."

To rescue her daughter she'd need a man who could find his way through cities and mountains alike...a man known to the law as "Mother." She had studied her choices and the best man was Duncan Tallchief. As a top researcher, she was rarely mistaken. "Mother" was the operative name for a man skilled at manhunting in the mountains or in the cities, and Duncan was especially gentle and loved by the children he rescued. Now, immersed in a brawl, he looked nothing like the tender, compassionate man in the children's reports.

Sybil closed her eyes as Duncan's tongue flicked out to taste the trickle of blood beside his hard mouth. His torn shirt exposed a hair-flecked, tanned chest, and every ounce of his lean body, which was packed into the standard cowboy outfit, surged with power. His rakish grin, showing a lurking dimple, could disarm a woman. He was a tough man, bred of the Wyoming elements, and just what she needed...when he wasn't having a good time brawling. He was massive and smart. She deplored the knowledge that this was the man who could rescue her child.

A chair skidded across the floor to her. She glanced at the men leisurely observing and commenting on the technical aspects of the fight. She recognized them from her research photographs. Duncan's brothers had the same sleek, black hair inherited from their Native American ancestor and gray eyes from their great-great-grandmother. The three of them could power-devastate most women. Sybil wasn't most women. She was clinical and cool and had hardened her heart against love. She glanced at the men lounging at the table. There was Birk, a race-car driver, rodeo star and builder. Calum, a professional hit man for businesses with problems, had the only neatly trimmed haircut. Fiona and Elspeth, the Tallchief sisters, weren't in sight.

In the pictures of the three brothers, Duncan had appeared the hardest, his expression like a closed door. The eldest brother and the major owner and manager of Tallchief Cattle Ranch should have been wearing spurs on his boots and low-slung Colt pistols on his hips. The younger brothers sheltered that dark and dangerous look, but Duncan wore it like a cloak.

A patrol car slid by the window and a search beam shot into the melee, outlining Duncan's head above the others. The stark, primitive power in a brawling male horrified Sybil. Maddy waved the car away and caught a liquor bottle on its way to his mirror.

Oh, fine. Here she was in Amen Flats, no more than a wide spot in the road, faced with settling a fight Tallchief clearly enjoyed. Sybil straightened her shoulders. She couldn't let Duncan Tallchief be beaten to a pulp; she didn't have the time for him to recover from broken bones.

Sybil stepped over one chair and another, making her way to the brothers. "Hello."

Two sets of masculine, gray eyes drifted over her expensive sweater and slacks. The Tallchiefs shared a look before returning their eyes to her.

"Well, hello."

Birk's deep voice held sensual interest that caused Sybil to stiffen. She didn't like to be peered at; she preferred to research and examine. Calum, a methodical man, studied her dark-red hair, pulled up and away from her face in a tight, neat knot. His gaze touched her large glasses, penetrating them to find her light-brown eyes and the slant of her cheekbones. Sybil knew her features ran more to plain than beautiful; she had been told the same often. She shifted restlessly and glanced at Duncan, who had just pushed a man away to get at a beefier man, Jack. Jack was raving about Duncan stealing his wife.

Sybil closed her eyes and lamented inwardly. Oh, fine. Oh, fine, oh, fine. . . . She had chosen a womanizer as her daughter's white knight.

Aware that the Tallchief brothers' sweeping study had taken in her tall, slender, long-legged body, Sybil turned to them. She detested the male interest. She wasted no time, because two men had grabbed Duncan's arms, supporting him for Jack's fists. Duncan's expression should have been fearful; it wasn't. He lifted his bruised lips for a kiss thrown in Jack's direction.

"He's outnumbered. I really think that you should help him," she stated in her best cool and logical voice.

"Nah. Duncan has them overmatched. I'm Birk. This is Calum. Sit down and enjoy the view."

"He's your brother," Sybil insisted, striving to remain calm and contain her rapidly growing anger. Here was the man she hoped would help her . . . the man her research had shown to be most proficient at the kind of work she needed done. Duncan Tallchief could be disabled or, worse, killed, and there wasn't another man her research had shown would be as effective.

"How do you know he's our brother?" Calum asked quietly, always the cool, dissective mind.

Sybil dismissed the question. The Tallchief brothers looked as though they were cut from the same arrogant mold, though Duncan looked fiercer. Of course, he was brawling and they hadn't lifted a finger to help him. Sybil pushed away a dram of sympathy for the massive man battling away at the bar. "I've come for Duncan. I want you to help him before he's disabled."

Birk's and Calum's matching frowns deepened. "Tell us more," Birk invited.

She dismissed his humor. "I don't have time for this. Duncan could be hurt. Are you going to help him or not?" Sybil demanded, pushing away a shiver of dark anger. When the brothers didn't move and the man, Jack, sank a ham-sized fist into Duncan's middle, Sybil shot Birk and Calum a look of sheer disgust. "Very well. I'll take care of it myself."

Both brothers stood instantly, looming over her. Each took an arm, their hold firm, yet gentle. "You could get hurt."

Sybil's research had shown that the brothers were too protective of women. They towered over her now like guardian angels. "Do something," she ordered, politely gripping their wrists and pushing lightly. She disliked being touched.

Calum and Birk released her and glanced at the fight. Birk nodded thoughtfully. "He's doing okay. Duncan doesn't usually like interference."

"Oh, he doesn't, does he?" Sybil closed her eyes, counted to ten and began to step over a chair on her way to help Duncan. A big hand latched on to the back of her sweater and began to reel her to safety. Because she had learned the hard way that women should protect themselves, Sybil unleashed her best martial-arts kick—tempering it a bit because the brothers meant well.

Birk grunted satisfactorily as she continued making her way to Duncan. She brushed back the long, curling mass of hair that had come unwound and now flew around her shoulders. She paused a moment thoughtfully, then tugged away her glasses and tossed them to Calum, who was grinning widely.

"I detest what I am about to do," she muttered grimly.

Duncan ducked another punch and caught sight of the tall woman making her way to him. She was glorious; long, red hair flying as she moved toward him. Her eyes flashed murderously, reminding him of topaz lit by fire.

He deliberately took a punch, reeling with it. The red-haired woman gracefully hopped over a chair. A Tallchief trait was playing to the audience and Duncan took another light punch and sagged, carefully watching the woman come to his rescue. Birk and Calum were standing, noting her progress. One wrong move from the men toward her and they would haul her back to safety. The woman continued mumbling darkly to herself. "You're hurting him," she said very properly. "I insist that you stop."

The five men paused, glanced her way and frowned, then leaped at Duncan.

"Very well. If you insist on violence . . ."

One of her kicks sent Lyle Maddox curling to the floor. A neat clip of her hand caught Bobby Law on the neck. She elbowed Henry's beer belly and sent a hand flying into Paul's face, bloodying his nose. She looked at her palm, grimaced and quickly dunked a napkin in a glass of water. She scrubbed her hand thoroughly and returned to her mission, all in a matter of seconds. Birk let out a guffaw just as she caught the flaccid muscle in Jack's shoulder and brought him to his knees.

She glared up at Duncan, who was observing her through one good eye and a slightly swollen one. He found himself grinning at her. "My heroine," he murmured, and watched fire ignite in her eyes.

They were light brown, he decided. Lit by flames of her temper.

She grabbed his torn shirt. He watched her hands tremble upon him, and was fascinated by her pale skin against his chest, exposed by the torn cloth. Her lips worked for a heartbeat before sound came.

"I detest violence. *You are to come with me, Duncan Tallchief.*"

Shivering in her temper, her freckles dancing across her skin and her lips tight with anger, the woman continued to glare up at him. He decided she was trying to shake him.

"Oh, fine," she muttered.

Her fingers fluttered over his face, checking the damage. Her expression lay between disgust and grim concern. He gave himself to those elegant fingers, as they gently touched his swollen eye and lip. She dabbed a napkin at the trickle of blood and leveled a dark look up at him.

"Shame on you."

He pushed a kiss at her fingertips and wanted to carry her off as his prize. As if he were her little boy, she tugged his torn shirt together, did up the remaining buttons and smoothed the cloth on his shoulder.

Duncan stood absolutely still, dazed by the idea that she was fussing over him.

God, she was lovely, her furious topaz eyes filling her face, the russet strands of her hair fiery against her pale skin. Duncan watched the rapidly beating pulse in her throat and saw the passion course through her slender body. Dressed in pale green, she reminded him of a cool fern—a delicate, lacy frond, quivering in a summer breeze. Then the tigress shifted within her, the image changing to a passionate huntress locked on to something she wanted badly.

Duncan went light-headed. He was the prize she sought. Heat skimmed across him, enveloped him as he stared at the curve of her mouth, untouched by color. Creams, reds, pinks, subtle golds danced and flashed around her, heightened by the cool green of her loose sweater and slacks. Duncan struggled against Jack's well-placed last punch and wondered how her lips would taste beneath his.

There was little he could do but wrap her against him and kiss her.

With one hand, he cupped the back of her head, fitting her to the kiss. He dived into the scent of her hair, which flowed around him, catching on the stubble of his cheek. Spice and flowers enveloped him. He pushed closer to the fire, the heat within. Against his body, hers was slender, strong and pliant. The nudge of her breasts against him sailed right into his desire, heavy needs that he hadn't allowed to escape for years....

Her mouth parted beneath his, a tender flower to be treated gently. He lifted his head and found softness lurking in her stunned gaze . . . before the fury came ripping back.

"How dare you . . ." she demanded.

She was livid with anger, and trembling with an urge Duncan recognized—the woman wanted to hurl herself at him and make him pay. He'd seen Fiona's temper often enough, and Elspeth's, too. Other women didn't fly at him; there was no reason they should.

"Thank you for rescuing me," he murmured, enchanted by the hot color rising up her cheeks. For her, he pushed the muscles around his lips into a rusty smile. He wondered if tigresses kissed bruised lips.

"Let me go," she whispered between her teeth.

He wondered how they would feel beneath his tongue.

Slowly, reluctantly, he released her. Because fear moved within the woman, shrouded her, reaching out to chill him after her first dazed reaction. He saw the fern again, quivering, hoarding pain. Dew glistened like tears on the fragile, lacy frond.

He mourned losing the soft movement of her lips against his, a kiss lost before it was truly given. The woman had known the worst of fear and was untutored in lovemaking . . . even now she wrapped her fury around her like a protective cloak. What had made her come to him, fight her way through a low-class tavern brawl, when clearly she was well-bred? He lingered on the question and enjoyed her simmering anger. He guessed it was a bit of the boy in him, rising to the surface after a brawl.

Birk hooted and Calum lifted his beer mug in a toast. "She's come for you, older brother."

"Is there somewhere we can talk?" the woman asked tautly, catching and donning the huge glasses Calum tossed to her.

Duncan mourned the shielding of her eyes, with their curious slant and reddish brown lashes. He realized she fought now to draw a colorless cloak around her, to return to the shadows and safeguard the vibrant woman within. Unwilling to release what he had touched a heartbeat ago, Duncan eased a willful russet strand of hair behind a well-formed ear devoid of jewelry.

Her eyes darted away. Clearly she was a woman unused to tenderness. Fear—worse, panic and desperation—rode her more than the need to be enclosed by shields and shadows. What had driven her to leave them?

She had spoken like a mother—"Shame on you."

Tenderness lurched within him, replacing the passion sweeping through him a moment ago. He carefully put his hand around her trembling one, sensing that she needed reassurance. She tensed, hesitating, weighing, then finally allowed him to hold her hand. Her cold hand was smooth, the slender, ringless fingers strong. The woman worked with her mind—he traced her fingertips lightly, just once, and found slight calluses. In those shadowy brown eyes was a desperation he'd seen before—when parents came to him, asking for help.

"What is it?" he asked quietly, placing a firm boot on the back of Jack's head as the man started to rise. "Take a note, Jack. I'm busy." Jack groaned and sank back onto the floor.

A very private woman, he decided, as she quickly glanced around the room. One who kept her pain to herself, but now must leave that safe shroud to expose herself to another—

"I'm going to my ranch now." It was an offer, quietly put, so as not to frighten her. "We can talk there." Would she come, or would fear anchor her?

When someone agreed too quickly to his terms, he knew the matter was not light.

She nodded. "I'll wait outside for you. I'll follow you in my car."

Duncan watched her move elegantly toward the door and close it softly behind her. No questions, no conditions. The woman was more desperate than he thought.

He steered his pickup slowly toward the mountains, keeping sight of her headlights in his mirror. The woman drove an expensive car, unsuited to the rugged road leading to his isolated ranch house. She drove skillfully, returning his flashing lights to signal she was all right. They circled the wind-tossed lake that had reminded his great-great-grandmother of Scotland, just as the jutting mountains had. Meadows and rich grazing land lay upon Tallchief Mountain like sprawling jewels among the rocks and pines. Duncan's small flock of sheep, a hairy Scottish breed, had adapted well to the mountains.

His rock-and-wood addition to the Tallchief house was new, built by him and his brothers. The spacious home nestled in the pines and jutted into the night sky. Elspeth's woven goods softened the wood interior with a few Native American artifacts. His great-great-grandfather's peace pipe lay on the roughly hewn mantel. The Tallchief's first branding iron lay beside it, the pattern of a stick man seared in barn wood. The dull red of a Sioux shield, decorated by feathers and porcupine quills, hung in the shadows.

Blood tied him to this raw, beautiful land. He was bred here, loved it. The woman would look fragile and pale inside his home. Duncan knew gossip would flame immediately, because more than a few women wanted to claim him. He'd been a celibate man since his divorce, yet none of them had stirred him like the woman tonight.

The woman who needed him, a woman of fire and shadows....

He left the front door ajar for her, then went to coax the wood furnace into life. He rarely used the comfort, but the woman needed warmth and a bit of care. Despite her well-groomed, expensive exterior, she seemed very lonely, as though untouched by concerned loved ones.

"They call you 'Mother.'"

When she referred to his code name, he understood why she was so desperate. Framed against the huge windows skimmed by the light, falling snow, she was too thin. Used to tracking with his senses, Duncan prowled through what he knew of her and what he felt. She was probably missing a child—

Duncan continued to prod the hearth's fire. The woman's knowledge was not shared by the townspeople. Duncan, too, had his secrets; he preferred not to expose them or to lose his effective shield. Keeping the newspapers at bay wasn't easy after the rescue of a wealthy child.

"We haven't been properly introduced," she said, confirming her good breeding. "I'm Sybil White. You're Duncan Tallchief and I need you...ah...that is...my daughter, Emily, has been kidnapped. We live in Seattle. I've traced her to this area. I'm...I'm pretty certain my ex-husband has her...at least the flight attendant's description fitted him.''

Straight to the point. Sybil hadn't glanced at his house, searching out bits of his privacy. Desperation left little space for idle curiosity.

Duncan rose slowly to his feet and realized that Jack's punch had bruised a rib. He rubbed his side, and behind the large glasses, Sybil's eyes darkened with a flash of impatience. Her eyes skipped down to his chest, lingered briefly on the whorls of hair, then moved away into the night. Across the room, she looked drained, shadows beneath her eyes. ''Let's talk in the kitchen,'' Duncan said, allowing her to follow him. ''I'm in the mood for a snack.''

She could do with food and rest. He began to heat stew laced with barley and vegetables. She stood very rigid, clasping a leather file holder to her as if nothing could tear it away. He saw in her a mother's fierce love and despair.

He saw in her a woman who could claim his heart.

The thought shook him to his boots. He'd had close relationships, but a woman like this one—wounded, vulnerable, holding pain within her—raised his protective instincts. That was his problem with women, Duncan brooded—his need to protect. Too often women misinterpreted that care for something else.

He preferred to keep to himself after he discovered how some women were drawn to him and he to them.

Marriage wasn't a dream he'd try again.

Duncan tugged a refrigerator magnet away and let it snap back. When it came to wounded women, he didn't have a callus to protect himself.

Duncan ran his hand over his jaw. But he hadn't known how vulnerable she was when she'd come like a tigress for him. Maybe he'd been flexing his muscles even as he saw her walk in, all cool and style, to the tavern. If that tigress appeared again, there would be a duel, because she touched sparks within him—a bit of boyish show-off and a deeper, primitive need.

Tension ran through him now, simmering and lodging heavily in his lower body.

That damned Tallchief kiss. He'd known he needed the fire of her mouth beneath his the moment she'd hopped over that chair....

Duncan used the excuse of a shower to take him to the privacy he required. Moments later, dressed in a worn, flannel shirt and jeans, Duncan padded on bare feet to where she ladled the stew into bowls. "So you're domesticated. That's a nice addition to martial-arts skills," he taunted her gently, aware of his own uncertainty.

She shot him a dark, moody look, dismissing his nudge to reveal something about her life. "You could have gotten hurt. Emily...we need you. If you think I liked my first debut into—"

She hesitated and some past horror wrapped itself around her. What was it? Duncan wondered.

She looked away and rubbed her hands as if they were chilled to the bone. "I detest physical violence."

He wanted to wrap his arms around her and tell her he would take care of her—that he would rescue her daughter. She pushed away her food and resented his insistent spooning of it into her mouth. For her, submission wasn't easy, but she wanted his help desperately and made the small concession.

Duncan's lower body hardened each time the spoon slid into her mouth.

"Any amount of money—" she began, only to be stopped by another rich spoonful.

Elspeth wasn't long in calling. After answering the phone impatiently because he didn't want to be distracted from the woman, Duncan scowled. He should take a dip in dignity, Elspeth advised tartly, and shot through a quick account gained from Birk and Calum.

"You've never taken a woman to your house, Duncan. You were showing off at Maddy's. Think of what people will say. If she needs a place to stay—"

"You'll be picking at whys and whats," he finished, used to Elspeth's caring tongue. "Maybe I want her here without your advice," he added to rile his sister's temper. "She stays with me."

"Poor woman. She hasn't a clue. Exactly what are you doing with her now?" Elspeth demanded, not to be put off.

"Why, I'm feeding her, dear sister. She's eating out of my hand," he returned in a drawl that always brought her temper soaring. He spooned another bite into Sybil's parted mouth, and patted the softness with a napkin. "Leave me alone with my rescuer, will you?" he asked before replacing the receiver in the cradle, none too gently.

He smiled grimly. Sybil reminded him of Elspeth, tall and elegant, with fire and steel running beneath. He thought of the woman coming to his rescue, the pampering and the petting, her fragile fingers smoothing his torn shirt. He was unused to that tenderness; it would do for a start....

"Show me what you've got," Duncan urged gently. "By the way, you realize that we are alone here and the situation could be..."

Again that flick of impatience, a woman with one goal in sight: the safe reclaiming of her daughter.

"I've investigated you. I'm a researcher, Mr. Tallchief—"

"'Duncan' to you," he interrupted, disliking the formality she placed between them. He wanted to rip it away, but thought better of it.

"Duncan. Very well. I'm a researcher and you are the best. Can you help me?"

He tilted his head and crossed his arms. To be investigated was a novelty. "So you've tapped into information only granted to lawmen. Interesting. You must be very skilled and desperate enough to play illegal games. What do you know about me?"

She preferred not to look directly at him, but studied her long, pale hands, instead. The sight of her slender fingers splayed open caused his heart to thud more quickly.

"Thirty-five. A cattle rancher with an interest in Scottish sheep and replenishing buffalo on the lower plains. You've lived here all your life. Lost your parents when you were eighteen and kept your younger brothers and sisters together. It couldn't have been easy. You're respected and active in community affairs. You could have a degree with all the courses you've taken—animal husbandry, environmental impact, wildlife—but you don't. You found a child when no one else could, and your wife left you shortly after. The court papers stated irreconcilable differences, I believe. Law officials call you 'Mother.' ''

"That's enough." Duncan didn't like anyone prowling through his private life, a marriage gone sour. He'd been filled with dreams when he walked into his marriage. He'd given his all to that marriage, but it hadn't been enough for Lauren. He'd hated the ugliness within him then, the desperation as the dreams died. Lauren had wanted to sell Tallchief Mountain for her share of the divorce and shouldn't have backed him into that corner. Protecting his family's heritage, he hadn't been nice. The divorce had been messy and had strangled a good amount of trusting women out of him. They were still friends, he and his ex-wife. He realized later that he'd wanted more than she could give; he'd wanted the deep love his parents had shared. He'd wanted a houseful of children, and it wasn't meant to be. At times the memory of what he'd wanted, his dreams, was too fresh—

The Tallchiefs were said to have their backbones forged in steel. . . .

"I'll help you." Duncan knew that whenever a child was taken, he would help if he could. He examined Sybil's files, forgetting her momentarily as he immersed himself in facts, dates, the suspect.

They were in his office now, studded with books, files and computers and overlooking the Wyoming night. Her scent caught him unawares just as he was prowling through the background material on her ex-husband. He slipped a disk into his computer and ran through more information. "I like your perfume," he said truthfully. "But you distract me."

"I do?" Her reaction was shocked, honest, a woman unaccustomed to male attention. "I'm not wearing perfume."

This time he was impatient. Sweeping her body with his eyes, he spared her nothing of his desire. "A woman's body has a scent of its own. I haven't been near a woman in a long time. There's enough tension in me to— Look, you can't be completely naive. Didn't anyone warn you about following men to isolated places?"

"But I . . ." She didn't finish, cut short by his dark look.

The flush rising from her throat caught him in the gut, turning it wickedly. A hard surge of desire ran through him, even as he recognized her pain. His tigress had scars all her own. "Tell me about yourself. Everything."

"I'm not interesting," she protested, that flag of anger rising in her topaz eyes. "Emily—"

"Take off your glasses," he ordered. "You're nearsighted. You only use them for distances anyway. I want everything you know and nothing shielding it."

"You are a demanding man."

Reluctantly, daintily, she removed her glasses. He admired her courage as she plopped them into their case. She placed them in a functional bag. Everything about her was neat and classic and expensive, from her large bag to her clothing. Despite her travel, she barely looked rumpled.

"Something isn't here," he said carefully as she sat by his side, examining the scrolling lines on his computer screen. He studied her face—the high, elegant forehead and the slight lines around her eyes; lines of fatigue were etched around the generous curve of her mouth. He studied her slightly squarish jaw and watched it tense; she didn't like his surveillance as he said, "Early thirties. Evidently with money and breeding. One child. Emily is how old? Thirteen? Your marriage to…Frank, wasn't it? Lasted six years? Who is Emily's father?" he asked, and watched Sybil pale instantly.

She shivered and looked out into the night. "I don't know the exact identity of Emily's father."

Duncan waited. She was too untouched, too fiercely protective of her body, to have given it easily or often. He was good at ferreting out gaps, but he sensed he wouldn't like this one. "I need everything, Sybil," he told her. "Or I can't help. Details leave a trail."

She closed her eyes, struggling to force the past from her. "I was raped. Emily's father could be any one of four boys…men now, I suppose."

Duncan reeled with that punch, more severe than the physical ones of the brawl. He saw a frightened young girl attacked by a gang, and with professional determination blocked the scene from his mind. He wanted to hold her against him, to soothe her— Instead he asked, "And your ex-husband? What was his relationship to Emily?"

"Strained. I...I am actually Emily's only parent. Her only relative. She's always depended entirely on me. She must be terrified now." Sybil's voice was low, haunted by fear and a little guilt. "It was three days before I got the note. Today is the fourth day. I spent time researching, locating the flight...finding you, a man called 'Mother.'"

"We'll locate her. It's just a matter of time." The circles beneath her eyes said she hadn't slept in days.

"You'll help me, then...to get Emily?" She needed his reassurance, her shadowed eyes begging him.

Duncan doubted that Sybil asked very much of the world; he would try his best to help her.

"Yes. Now, leave me alone," he said too gruffly, covering the tenderness he felt for this woman. Experience told him that every moment lost was dangerous to the girl. "Get some sleep. You can use one of the bedrooms upstairs."

"I'll stay here," she returned firmly. "You might need me. I've already tried researching the sources available."

"On the couch, then, and you don't have my resources. And by the way, Miss Light-fingers...keep your nose out of my private business," Duncan ordered, admitting a reluctance to let her leave him. He wanted to hold her against him, protect her and tell her her child would be safe. But he'd found two children who hadn't lived, and he wasn't offering false hopes.

She shivered, crossing her arms and digging her fingers into the knit sweater. "I am sorry. I realize the value of privacy."

He felt as if he'd slapped her, and she looked as if she'd already been battered. Duncan cursed himself silently. "You did what you had to do. Lie down on the couch. It's comfortable." The thought of her sleeping in one of his beds nettled him. Unused to the fierce tug of desire, Duncan began working quickly, tapping keys, finding sources, tracking....

Two

Sybil dozed, cuddling warm softness closer to her...her baby was her sunshine, her world. Emily was a special part of her, the best part, renewing Sybil's faith in family love. From the first moment she'd discovered her pregnancy, she'd loved Emily desperately. When Emily was placed into her arms, the pain within Sybil had settled. . . .

Wrapped in a half sleep, she found Duncan's eyes at a level with her own. In the lamplight, his face was all rugged angles and harsh lines. Textures of tanned and weathered skin blended with blue-black hair. Light glistened on the raven stubble covering his unrelenting jaw. She looked away from the shadowy heat in his eyes, the pulse beating slowly in his well-muscled throat. Duncan Tallchief was a very physical man, just the sort of man she avoided . . . not safe relationship material at all.

The huge dog at his side watched her with unblinking white eyes. "This is Thorn. Part malamute, part wolf and the rest mean yellow dog."

"Thorn." Sybil held very still. The dog appeared the perfect match for a man like Duncan, fierce and savage. Then the animal lowered his head to nudge her hand.

Duncan's expression was sheer disgust. "He wants you to pet him. Elspeth and Fiona have spoiled him rotten. He thinks all women should cater to him."

Sybil scratched the dog's ears and he preened, turning to let her rub his throat. Master and dog were more well suited than Duncan knew.

She caught a fresh, grassy scent wrapped in smoke. Duncan's eyes revealed little as he jerked his head to smoke rising from a large, flat dish with Native American designs. "I meditate sometimes."

She studied his angular face, his lean cheeks and shadowy eyes. There was more to the man than the hunter.

"I uncovered a lead," he said quietly.

"What is it?" Then she caught the fresh scent of soap, wood smoke and leather on him. He was no dream—but a grim hunter. She came fully awake. "You're going after her now, aren't you?"

He nodded, the lamplight flickering across his straight, black lashes. His bruised eye was only slightly swollen now. She realized that during the night, he had placed a heavy blanket over her and had removed her shoes.

Emily! She flung back the blanket and jammed her feet into her shoes. "I'm going with you."

"Frank left a trail of credit-card expenditures, including renting a car from the airport. He purchased camping gear and rented horses for trail riding. That was in Ridge Point, ten miles from here. He asked directions for a line cabin up in the mountains. He had a young girl with him and said she was his daughter. The girl didn't talk. He's probably threatened her."

Sybil stared at Duncan. "I couldn't get any information from the car-rental people. How did you find out?"

He drew on a heavy shearling coat over his black sweater. He looked lethal, his face hard and his gray eyes wintry. An anger ran beneath his cold expression, an anger that would serve to track Emily. In another time, he would have frightened Sybil. But she knew instinctively that Duncan was determined to find her child. She could trust him, as she had trusted few people in her lifetime.

"I have friends. I'll bring her back. Four days, maybe five. The sheriff knows what's happening and who to look for. They've given me five days' head start. The sheriff will be waiting for word of Emily. His number is near the phone. Keep in touch with him."

Fifteen minutes later he was closing the pickup door after her. Within the shield of his hat brim and his turned-up collar, his eyes were narrowed into slits and definitely unwelcoming. "Women" was all he said as Sybil, dressed in his jacket, had piled into the pickup. Two horses waited in the trailer behind the truck.

Between them on the bench seat, the dog turned white eyes from master to her. She hugged the dog, needing the reassuring warmth. Duncan glanced at her before turning the key. "Show them to me."

"What?" This man was not the happy brawler of the previous night, or the gentle one who had awakened her. With his coat collar tucked up around his jaw, his face shadowed and taut beneath the low brim of his western hat, he could have been a killer. A man to be feared.

But she didn't fear him. He would help her. She knew it.

His eyes flashed, the color of winter light on steel. "The damned long johns, that's what. You're not going without them."

She forced a tight, triumphant smile and unbuttoned her shirt to show the silky, thermal underwear. He nodded and looked meaningfully at her jeans. Without hesitation, Sybil jerked open the snap and slid down her zipper.

For an instant, she was horrified by her reaction—her opening her clothing for his inspection. But they were bound together, this man and her, to find Emily. Little else mattered. What he wanted, needed, to know she would give him. Anything to help her daughter. *Emily....*

"Good." Duncan reached for her ankle, wrapped his fingers around her boot and drew it onto the steering wheel. Thorn watched with interest as Duncan tugged back her jeans leg. He found the top of her boot and probed inside to her heavy stockings. "Italian boots on a Wyoming mountain.... But you put on my stockings. They're silk and good insulation."

Sybil dismissed the slight trembling, even as the fear of being touched rose within her. She'd chosen the right man.

Hours later, Duncan rode his horse ahead of her, glancing back through the mountain's morning mist to seek her. Wrapped in his coat, his scents, Sybil admitted needing his strength.

A loner, she rarely made friends, and this man had taken her lips as though placing a claim on her. She'd had most of her life laid out for her by people with claims. She preferred loneliness.

Draining hours later, the dog rested his muzzle across her legs and she stroked his ears. She prayed for Emily and hated Frank. Freezing mist settled on the knit hat she wore and penetrated her clothing to chill her. She was unused to riding a horse, and her muscles protested.

"How do you know this is where Frank took her?" Sybil asked, the fatigue draining her. *Emily . . . please be safe. I love you, honey.*

Duncan glanced over his shoulder, then scowled. He crouched beside the campfire, cooking their meal. The campfire lit his face, all angles and planes, glistening on his beard and on the sleek black of his hair. Sybil saw the warrior in him, the fierce line of his cheekbones gleaned from his chieftain ancestor. Beneath slashing brows, his eyes flickered over her as she sprawled on the sleeping bag, too tired to remove her boots. Duncan stripped them away. The dog stood, shook himself and moved to curl up on a saddle blanket.

A woman used to living alone with her daughter, Sybil resented Duncan's care. She was always the strong one, the one in charge. His efficiency both nettled and soothed her. Duncan left no doubt that he was disgusted by taking her, yet he wouldn't deny her the smallest comfort.

She hadn't asked him for anything but her daughter's safe return. Schooled at covering her emotions, Sybil avoided Duncan's level, too-astute gaze. He began to rub her legs, which now felt like logs after a day in the saddle. Here he was, strong in his element, while she was helpless. She knew books and computer files, not the touch of a man. Frustration and fatigue tore at her as she jerked her leg away from his strong, massaging hands. She'd been held down and—

Duncan quickly retrieved her ankle and circled it loosely with his fingers. None too gently, he yanked her legs across his and began massaging them. "Do you know that I've never allowed any woman to bully me?" he demanded between his teeth. "Look at you. You're undernourished, half dead with lack of sleep. You'll eat every drop in your bowl, understood?"

"I haven't complained, have I? I've followed every order you've shoved down my throat, haven't I? I'll keep up. I'm stronger than I appear." She hated the arrogant way he tossed out orders, expecting her to obey.

He loosened her single, long braid, then ran his fingers through it. "Right." He didn't sound as if he believed her. "You're really up for camping, aren't you? You're wearing Italian boots with thin soles on Wyoming rocks, lady. Why didn't you ask your family for help?"

"They wouldn't give it," she answered truthfully, feeling empty. She'd begged them once to love her daughter. They couldn't be bothered with a child spawned during a rape... rather, the tawdry affair they'd thought she'd had. They hadn't believed her tale of the well-bred boys attacking her that night. She was lying, they'd insisted. The old-money society families couldn't possibly allow her lies, her mother had said in a quiet, cold way.

No... she wouldn't give her baby away....

Duncan, looking more like an outlaw than a rescuer, brought their bowls to the sleeping bag. They ate quietly and Duncan insisted Sybil clean her plate. He ignored the angry flick of her eyes. "We'll find Emily. There is only one place on the mountain that Frank will go. From the camping gear he bought, he isn't skilled at roughing it."

He placed his arm around her shoulders, and for once Sybil accepted the comfort. "She's all right," he reassured her.

"You don't know Frank. He delights in tormenting the helpless." Sybil fought the tears rising in her eyes, burning her lids. She never cried, not since... Then Duncan was lifting her, placing her on his lap and shoving her face into the warmth of his throat. She struggled for an instant, then sank into the shelter he offered. Few people had given her a safe harbor, nor had she asked them to. Now, raw with worry and fatigue, she desperately needed the refuge. She clung to him, digging her fingers into his coat. "I'm so scared," she whispered, shocked that she was crying against his skin, letting him hold her like a child.

"What about your family? Where are they?" Duncan asked gently, stroking her hair. She listened to the steady beat of his heart and wondered why she let him hold her. . . .

Alone on the mountain, nestled against a man she barely knew, Sybil found herself voicing a raw pain that had torn at her for years. "They . . . they can't accept Emily. She doesn't exist for them. . . ."

"We'll find her," Duncan repeated slowly, rocking her.

She fell asleep to the sound of his heart, each beat bringing her closer to Emily.

Frank's capture and the recovery of Emily were easier than Duncan had believed. Frank, an inexperienced woodsman, had lit a roaring fire in the old cabin. The smoke brought Duncan and Sybil to him. Frank had known he was no match for Duncan and submitted easily. He'd begged them not to set Thorn on him; the dog had been baring his fangs and growling, his hackles raised.

All cool grace, Sybil had walked over to Frank. His sneer dropped as Sybil looked at him. He shouldn't have laughed in her face, Duncan decided. She had leveled Frank to a groveling ball curled on the frozen earth. When their offspring were threatened, mothers could be very effective in their rage. Later they were usually shocked—Duncan knew that Sybil had probably never used her knee so effectively as she had against Frank.

Duncan had tucked the girl against him and leaned back against a tree. "Princess, your mother is choosing a method of therapy she'll probably regret. But maybe we'd better let her get it out of her system. A release sort of thing."

The girl had huddled against him. "I knew she'd find me," Emily whispered. "My mother is special."

Duncan believed it. Sybil had shaken herself and stepped back, contemptuous of the fallen man. Clearly embarrassed, she'd straightened her clothing with shaking hands. "Emily, dear. I'm sorry for that. I detest violence."

To the girl's credit, she'd managed a shaky grin. "No television for you tonight, Mom."

Duncan laughed outright and tapped Sybil's nose. The tigress flashed in her before it was concealed; she steamed magnificently.

"You!" she muttered, as if he'd caused her to release her revenge.

Duncan bent to brush his lips across hers, needing the taste of her to satisfy him that she was safe. He wanted her to know that they'd found her child and now all bets were off. The flames leaped within her at the caress of his lips over hers; a hurricane brewed—sultry, hot and unpredictable—before she jerked away.

Emily began to giggle, out of nervousness at first and then with growing humor. "Mom, you look—"

"I think she's cute," Duncan murmured, watching Sybil steam, the color rising in her throat.

"My mom?" Emily asked, shocked, her eyes wide.

Elspeth had claimed Sybil and Emily the moment Duncan brought them into Amen Flats.

She'd taken the White females under her wing, showing them Amen Flats, and Duncan resented Elspeth's interference. He was driven to tossing pebbles at Sybil's window after five days and nights of Elspeth's hoarding of them.

There wasn't a moment of those five days when Duncan wasn't damning himself for wanting to see Sybil White again. For wanting to hold her....

She had scars written all over her and he'd had his share of hard times, a broken heart. He was a fool for thinking twice about her.

Sybil appeared at the window, scanning the night, and Duncan stepped from the shadows of the pines. "Come down," he whispered, not happy about his need to see her.

He'd watched her sleep in his arms, and she wasn't aware of him as a man. That irked him.

"I'll see you tomorrow," she whispered back, framed by the open window. Her hair caught the moonlight, the chilling wind lifting it around her pale face.

"Like hell," Duncan told her, not to be put off by a woman who intrigued him. Few women had set terms for him. Sybil White was far too cool. "Get down here—now."

"I'm done following your orders, Duncan Tallchief. You're arrogant—"

Sybil threw a book at him and he caught it, smirking into the night. The moonlight lit Sybil's shocked expression, her hand covering her mouth. He leaned against an old shed and stared at the moon, mocking himself and his need to see her again.

Sybil, dressed in a black sweater and slacks, her magnificent mane of hair catching the moonlight, marched toward him. He admired the length of her stride, the square set of her shoulders. She hit his chest with a mass of his borrowed clothing. "There. I suppose you came for these. Though I don't know why you couldn't show up at a reasonable hour. Your sister is so caring I don't want to disturb her. We've already caused her so much inconvenience."

He placed a fingertip on her nose, entranced by her snit. This is how he wanted her: with the cool, perfect shroud torn away. "She loves mother-henning.... But what if I came for you?" he asked.

"Emily and I are very well," she said politely, although his drawl had widened her eyes. She shifted restlessly and shoved back a swath of willful hair. "Thank you."

"Did you miss me?" Duncan wanted to draw her into his arms, to take that sassy mouth beneath his and make her pay for his wild emotions. He moved to block the chilling wind from her and to better let the moonlight stroke her face.

Her eyebrows lifted. He saw her prowl through the proper returns before she said very carefully, "I am grateful to you."

He strolled a fingertip down her cheek and tapped her bottom lip gently. "It's not your gratitude I want."

She frowned, then shook her head. "Oh...oh, yes, of course. I should write you a check. I've been so busy with Emily. Frank is very good at demeaning. This time with Elspeth is helping. She's very good at making us feel special."

"Yes." Duncan remembered Frank's ravings before the tape had sealed his mouth shut. Emily, a quiet, well-mannered child, had been stunned by Duncan's quick dealing with Frank. She had giggled softly as Duncan swooped her up in his arms and tossed her lightly on his horse. The girl was too fragile, nothing more than white skin covering angular bones, and Duncan had fallen under her spell immediately. Perhaps it was because Emily had her mother's intelligence and her shyness. Or maybe it was because he was a sucker for children who looked as though they had taken too many of life's subtle punches.

The mother had also taken more than her share. But fire danced between Duncan and her, like a sword quickly lifted at a word, a look. His instincts told him that in the end, he would fight to have her, and not in a brotherly relationship, either.

Anger wrenched Duncan's gut. Sybil had roused him from his privacy and dared to tempt him. Now she wanted to pay him off and send him on his way. A Tallchief didn't walk away from something he wanted . . . not just yet. "A check," he repeated flatly. He chose to switch the raw subject. "How's Emily?"

"Wonderful. You're her hero. Birk and Calum dropped by, and between the three of you calling her 'Princess,' she's half in love. She's calling you and your brothers her three Black Knights." Sybil tossed back the strand of hair the wind had whipped across her lips.

"She is special. But so is her mother." Unable to wait longer, Duncan leaned down to brush a kiss across her mouth, startling her.

She was unused to tender touches. Her fingers hovered across her mouth, and then she shook her head. "Thank you again for Emily," she whispered, before running back into the house.

Duncan slammed his open hand against the fence. He'd frightened her.

The next morning Elspeth called to say that Sybil and Emily had gone.

By kidnapping Emily, Frank had sought a hefty ransom. Instead he received a trial and was sentenced to prison. At the trial Sybil avoided Duncan, and though irritated, he let the matter go. She needed healing . . . for the moment. The tracker's instinct within him told him that there would be another time.

Christmas passed and Duncan traced Sybil to Seattle. He investigated the basic elements of her life—where she lived and her work—and disliked himself for doing it. He had to know she was safe.

Elspeth didn't look up from her notes as the kitchen door slammed and a blast of January wind lifted the lace at her throat. "Shut the door, Duncan. I can't afford to heat the world."

"She sent me a thank-you note and a fat check." He tossed his snow-frosted hat to a chair and ripped away his heavy winter coat. Duncan sprawled on a chair and glared at Elspeth. Here in her soothing home filled with delicious aromas and calming colors, she looked too much at peace to suit him. "A damned note."

"I presume you are brooding about Sybil." Elspeth arranged the drawings she had been making from Una Fearghus's descriptions. The journals of the Tallchiefs' great-great-grandmother told of the loss of her Scottish dowry; as children the Tallchiefs had pledged to find Una's treasures. Elspeth pushed the drawing of a handmade cradle at Duncan, a circular Celtic design carved in the wood. Elspeth smiled, used to the quick moods of her family. "Una said that the woman who brought the cradle to a man of Fearghus blood would fill it with his babies."

"Prod one of the others, will you? I've been around that bend. It didn't work." Duncan stared sightlessly at the drawing. Thoughts of the cradle no longer brought the pain they once had after his divorce. His dreams had died slowly, futilely gasping for life during that time. The quest for the cradle belonged to the past, back when the Tallchief children were struggling against fate.

Duncan glanced around Elspeth's home, at her weaving studio looming off the kitchen. Mourning their parents and fighting the world, the Tallchief clan had plotted to return Una's dowry to the family. The ink in her journals was blurred when she described how the dowry had been sold to keep Tallchief Mountain and the ranch safe. The mountains were enough to remind her of Scotland, she wrote...her dowry was nothing compared with her love for the chieftain who had captured her. And whom she had tamed to a loving husband. So the dowry was sold in bad times and Una had cried.

Calum the cool was to retrieve Una's garnet ring, a gift from her grandmother. Birk the rogue was to find the rocking chair; its dainty wooden design was Una's inheritance from her brother, who was also an indentured servant in the new land. Elspeth the elegant tended Una's journals, and had begun creating designs from Una's detailed descriptions. Elspeth had pledged to retrieve the fine woolen paisley shawl, and Fiona the fiery, the youngest Tallchief, was to find Una's sewing chest filled with crochet hooks and baby shawls.

Duncan traced the circular Celtic design of the cradle. He'd tried to recover the heirloom and had failed. "I'm not in the mood for legends. The original one she brought to this country was burned for firewood by the people holding her papers. Tallchief carved another cradle from Una's drawings."

"She still considered it a part of her dowry. Tallchief recognized that she would not come to him without it. He carved another and arranged for his father to give it to her. Eat another cookie and tell me about Wyonna. Does she like her new life, her new job?"

"She's happy. She's gotten a grant and is studying abuse situations while she works. When the women's shelter is done, she'll be ready to help others." Without Jack's unkind attention, Wyonna was blossoming; her strength grew each day. Duncan had tucked her away and found her a job she liked. But Wyonna had grown up in Amen Flats and she wanted to return. If she did, she'd have to face Jack, and it would be with Duncan's protection.

Duncan frowned, remembering Frank's futile threats to Sybil. Frank had said he knew things—a kidnapper searching out the possibility of blackmail. From the stiff way she'd looked at him, head high and topaz eyes glowing in her pale face, Sybil no longer cared and Frank had known it. He'd pushed too hard and lost.

"Thanks to you. You're very good at defending the helpless, Duncan. And a disaster as a gentleman. I'm afraid my brothers inherited a bit of our great-great-grandfather's wild temper. And Fiona, too." Elspeth shoved a freshly baked cookie into his mouth. "For sweetness. You gave Sybil the

Tallchief kiss the first moment you met her. Latched your lips to hers and took. There you were, brawling at Maddy's and loving it.... Tossing pebbles at my windows. You break one of them while you're woman hunting and I'll make you pay and replace it. You frightened her, Duncan. Sybil's life hasn't included moonlight trysts or Black Knights or warriors capturing her."

She leveled a look at him. "I'm afraid you have inherited your share of our great-great-grandfather's attitudes toward women."

Duncan munched on the cookie and ran the back of his hand across his mouth. That kiss had haunted him, caused him nights of lost sleep. During the trip up the mountain, he'd thought only of the child's safety and prayed. But Sybil's kiss had lingered, stirring him, and his brotherly notions had fallen at his boots.

He wondered how she could have married a man like Frank. How had he hurt her? There were other scars left by an unforgiving family, and Duncan shook his head. He had his share of pain and had decided to leave marriage to those who were braver than himself. Tangling once with a woman he loved desperately could last him a lifetime. Once, he'd wanted a family to wrap around him; had wanted the loving that the Tallchiefs shared. Duncan and Lauren had been two separate halves that should have grown together. But when the white-hot heat of youth began to cool, they were still separate.

Looking back, Duncan could see the ill-match that had lasted only a year. Lauren had needed a gentler man, and she found one, having two children in short order.

Duncan toyed with the woven place mat in front of him, circling the Celtic design. Pride kept him from going after Sybil, waylaying her and kissing her with the hunger that lurched each time he thought of her. To protect himself from Elspeth's sharp intuition about his need of Sybil, he asked absently, "How's Fiona?"

"She's in Arizona, and you know very well she's fighting land sale con-men. You're mooning for Sybil, Duncan. Admit it," Elspeth prodded, jotting down another note, this time a recipe. "She's got you. There you were, a lonesome old wolf, tried and failed at marriage, settling in that mountain castle like a hermit—''

"Lay off," Duncan ordered lightly. "My social life is none of your concern."

Elspeth ran an elegant hand up to smooth her sleek, black chignon and Duncan thought of Sybil's wild, red hair as she'd leaped across the barroom chair. He studied Elspeth beneath his lashes and watched her knowing smile. Elspeth placed her thumb against his, tiny scar to scar. "I could leave you alone to mold. But I won't. As the eldest sister, it's my right to torment you and see you safely tucked under the care of another woman. I'm doomed until then."

Duncan leveled a glare at Elspeth. "You're sticking up for her, aren't you?"

Elspeth met his hard eyes with her softer ones and grinned. "She hasn't a clue about you. She doesn't know how beastly you can be. I do. I've seen you at your worst. You've bullied me my entire life. Only because I've let you. You can't just sweep down off your mountain and expect her to be glad— imagine, tossing pebbles at my windows. Now, eat another cookie and go pick on someone else. I've got a loom that needs feeding."

Sybil tucked the shelving paper into place and began stacking dishes in the cabinet. She'd had to leave Seattle; she'd felt too vulnerable there after the kidnapping. She'd wanted a new beginning for herself and for Emily. Because she could think of no place safer, and because she had nowhere else to go, she'd come back to Amen Flats and to Elspeth's gentle friendship. Emily, her red hair tied in a ponytail and a fresh batch of freckles dancing across her nose, grinned up at her mother. "I'm going to love going to public school in Wyoming. Do you think we can go to the rodeos this summer? Maybe I could compete? Huh, Mom? Maybe barrel-race?"

"We'll see. You'll have to learn how to ride first."

"Duncan will teach me. I know he will. Elspeth says that all the Tallchiefs can ride like demons. She said that only the Tallchief men could have ridden after their parents' killer. She said that she thinks Tallchief men might have a touch of the devil in them. She said that right in front of Birk and told him not to snarl about Lacey, her friend.''

Emily shifted gears, her expression delighted. ''Or maybe Birk or Calum will teach me to ride. I've never been a part of a family before, Mom. But if Birk and Calum and Duncan are too old to be my brothers, then they can be my uncles, huh? They call me 'Princess' and sometimes I really think I am special—when they say it. I'm hoping that since I've never called anyone 'Dad' that Duncan might—''

She grinned hopefully when her mother seemed to be mustering a protest. She'd plagued Sybil about Duncan's light kiss after the rescue and innocently lit her mother's smoldering temper. Emily had never seen her mother truly angry except with Frank on the mountain. Yet the mere name Duncan Tallchief set her mother off nicely. Emily loved to tease Sybil about the man who looked like a desperado and had the gentle touch of one who cared. All thin arms and long legs, Emily ran out the screen door. Her laughter flowed after her, curling around Sybil. ''Gotcha, Mom!''

Sybil smiled; her daughter had completely forgotten the few days of Frank's mental abuse and was flowering nicely. The move to Amen Flats was exactly what she'd needed. Computers, overnight delivery and facsimile machines allowed Sybil to research wherever she lived; her work ran to genealogy and investigation of antiques, the location of desired articles. If she had to travel to her sources, Elspeth was ready to watch Emily.

The two cool, precise women had quickly become friends. Through the eldest Tallchief sister, Sybil had grown to like Birk and Calum and Fiona. Elspeth was nothing like her volatile, arrogant and playful brothers and the two women had corresponded since Emily's recovery. Elspeth's quiet, nurturing friendship filled an emptiness within Sybil and she had decided to move to the town that Elspeth had grown up in and loved so much. Sybil decided to wrap Emily in the close-knit community, something she'd never had. Sybil's fingers trembled on the dainty teacup. She released the china, pushing away her family's coldness. She desperately wanted Emily to have the warmth she'd discovered in the small town.

The homey, sunlit kitchen was perfect, gleaming and airy, nothing like the sterile ones at the mansion and her uptown, high-security apartments. The small house had a yard and space for a garden. Sybil had never lived in a real house and this one had a spacious front porch and a screened back one. Emily was already planning to plant flowers, and adopt a kitten and a puppy, her first pets. The rooms were plain and the bedroom she'd converted into an office was open and light. The house soothed Sybil, with its spreading shade trees and calming view of the mountains.

Warm, tender hearts resided in Amen Flats and half of them had welcomed her. Elliot Pinkman had mowed her yard and turned up the old flower bed. Lisa Brown and her friends had popped in with plant starts and cookies and casseroles. Children played on the sidewalk, shooting curious glances at Emily, who now wore a constant grin and acted as though every day were Christmas.

Duncan was another matter. He ignited Sybil's mild temper—she'd actually thrown a book at him—and the memory that she had slept in his arms on the trail disturbed her. Duncan could be tender and playful with children, but running beneath his quiet looks were steel and a brooding darkness she didn't understand.

He'd touched her as a brother on their way up the mountain, comforting, holding her.

After the brawl at Maddy's, he'd touched her as a man, kissed her. Wrapped her to his hard, warm length and placed his lips upon hers as though staking his claim. She'd thought of that kiss constantly, the brush of his lips across hers, seeking. The scents of his body tormented her; the texture of his unshaven chin snagged on her memories. Despite the brevity, the light possession, there was nothing cool about the kiss. Rather, it spoke of summer heat and male demands—

She'd had her share of male demands—much too rough, the hurting and the taking.

She'd had time to think, to remember how solitary Duncan's home was, softened only by patches of Elspeth's loom work and bits of Native American crafts and artifacts. He'd swept through the shadowy interior like a warlock, a dangerous male at home in his lair. He'd been hurt—she'd seen it in his eyes when she'd recalled his divorce. Then a steel door had slid closed, barring her from his secrets.

Despite his seemingly open life, Duncan was a man of secrets, hoarding them.

A woman would have to be a fighter to meet Duncan on a fair plane. Sybil had done all the fighting she wanted, from her cradle to the last cool, well-barbed argument about her leaving Seattle for the wilds of Wyoming. The Whites' eldest daughter had been marred; she'd ignored her duty to dispense with the illegitimate baby.

Sybil shivered just once, placing Duncan's storms and heat and her family's chill aside as she arranged her teacups in the cupboard. The screen door crashed behind her, and with a reprimand for Emily on her lips, Sybil glanced over her shoulder.

Duncan leaned against the kitchen counter, appearing just as dangerous as when she'd last seen him.

He was everything she'd never wanted in her life. Everything she didn't understand. Storms and lightning and tingles. Just looking at him, she knew the arrogant stance dried her mouth and lifted her temper. Or was it her temperature?

He raised a black eyebrow as she stared at him. "So you're back."

There was the dark, rough tone, accusation running through it. His gray eyes flickered down her loose, brown sweater and slacks.

"Duncan, how nice to see you..." she began, and stopped when he walked slowly to her, looming over her.

Suddenly the spacious, sunlit kitchen was too small. Dressed in a low-fitting western hat, a battered shirt and dirty, worn jeans and boots, Duncan looked as he had when they'd returned from the mountain. The muscle in his jaw rhythmically contracted and released, his day-old stubble gleaming. A spear of black hair shot across his forehead as he whipped off his hat and tossed it to the counter. "Miss me?" he demanded.

The low, dangerous purr of his voice lifted the hair on her nape.

Sex. Everything about Duncan Tallchief said he wanted her, from his sultry expression to the heat of his body. She'd been forced into sex and found it ugly.

"I...I...it is nice to see you." Sybil's hand went to her throat, shielding the fast-beating pulse. With Duncan she felt she needed shields and swords.

Duncan's eyes flicked to the movement and his hard mouth tightened. "So much for etiquette. I didn't like the check. Or your note."

"Wasn't it enough? According to my bank statement, the check hasn't been cashed. I'll write another one...." Sybil began to move around Duncan, but he placed his hands on the counter beside her hips.

"I tore it up. Rude of me, wasn't it?"

He was too close, and her breath came in gasps. Amusement glimmered in his eyes and curled on his lips. He was taunting her with something she didn't understand, yet feared. His thumbs stroked the curve of her hips; his flickering look dared her to toss away her manners.

Sybil inhaled and straightened. She did not like to be the butt of anyone's amusement. "Step back, please," she whispered as he continued studying her, from the tight knot on the top of her head down to the pounding pulse in her throat. She tried to breathe and failed, forced to tilt her head back to look up at him. She told him with her eyes how much she disliked his scrutiny.

"So you've moved to town," he drawled, inspecting her mouth. "*My* town." He might as well have said "My kingdom." "Now, let's see just how cool you really are."

Sybil found her lips were moving; she wished her brain would start turning again. Duncan's searing look had stopped it. She heard herself say, "Elspeth has been so kind. There were others...after we got back. I couldn't believe it. Emily never stopped talking about the people here—"

Emily had never stopped talking about *Duncan*, idolizing him. Sybil glanced over his shoulder to find Birk grinning at her.

"Duncan. Elspeth sent me. She's afraid you'll frighten our Miss Muffett away," Birk drawled. "Hello, Syb. I'm glad you've moved here. When you feel like playing tourist, give me a call. I'm in the book."

"Get out," Duncan returned easily, without unlocking his stare from hers. "Sybil-belle was about to tell me how much she missed me."

Feeling slightly guilty, fearing that Birk could sense the sensual tension hurtling off his brother, Sybil stood on tiptoe to look around Duncan's shoulder. "Stay and have cake."

Birk sniffed the air. "Chocolate with chocolate frosting? Don't mind if I do."

"I taught you how to drive, remember? How to shave and pitch a knuckleball," Duncan murmured, pulling rank. "Don't you have a building to level or a race to run?" Duncan said slowly before turning to his brother. He glanced at the white paint in Birk's hair and smirked. His brother had always had problems with one female. "Tangling with Lacey MacCandliss again?"

"Lacey hasn't learned that I'm her better. I've come to welcome Sybil to Amen Flats," Birk returned, the proud angle of his jaw matching his brother's.

Inches beneath the brothers' warring gray eyes, Sybil blinked as if she didn't believe the scene.

"Dibs."

The word curled from Duncan's mouth, softly and firmly. Sybil frowned, not understanding. She frowned again, and slowly remembered that "dibs" meant Duncan had claimed her... claimed her as his. *His? His what?*

"Yours?" Birk asked lightly with a grin. "How interesting. I thought you had rusted away up in your castle. Guess I'll be going, then." He tipped his hat to Sybil and winked at Duncan, who scowled back.

"Dibs? I hope that doesn't mean what I think it does," Sybil said when she could speak. She wanted to throw the chocolate cake at him.

Duncan slid his hands into his back pockets and tilted his head. His rangy, broad shoulders shifted, straightened. "You kissed me back. I'd say that said something."

It took Sybil a full two heartbeats to understand that Duncan had placed his claim upon her. *From the moment they'd met!* She fought the slow curling of heat up her throat and the press of her fists against her thighs. "No."

Temper flickered through Duncan's stormy eyes and was gone. "Don't write another check, Sybil-belle, or we'll tangle. You might not like the result."

She went very still, panicked by his dark, intimate look. "Please don't call me pet names. I really don't like it and I always pay my debts."

She fought the next words and lost. They leaped out of her like a hungry trout going for bait. "Especially to a muscled show-off who swaggers and enjoys brawling. By the way, I do not appreciate the research you did after I returned to Seattle. I'm not the only one with light fingers. You—Mr. Tallchief—apparently are quite the computer 'hacker'—you had a nice little stroll through my computer, didn't you?"

Anger lurched and flamed before Duncan shielded his gray eyes from her. His smile was cold, matching his eyes. "That would be Calum. And no, we're not in cahoots. Calum likes all the pieces to fit and yours don't. He's got the notion that Frank isn't done with you, especially after your testimony at his trial. You have an upscale clientele who request repeat performances, meaning you must be good. You're underpaid at times, proving you are a tenderhearted romantic after all."

While she fumbled with an accusation gone wrong, he nabbed a word and tossed it to her. "Swagger?"

"I'll deal with your brother later." Her temper flared. She'd learned a hard lesson and rarely met men in dangerous situations. Duncan was a dangerous man, yet she didn't fear him. She preferred to take him down a notch. "You saunter, Duncan. Swagger. Strolling in tight jeans as if you owned the world. That loose-legged walk with your shoulders—"

Duncan latched on to that, his beautiful mouth curving and the dimple in his cheek appearing.

"So you noticed my backside. Things are looking up. Yours is nice, too. A little more rounded than the last time I saw you." His gaze leisurely drifted down her body, warming it.

"Leave me out of your dreams, cowboy." Sybil's retort surprised her, but she held her ground as Duncan glared down at her. No one, but no one, had ever commented on her backside.

The morning air sizzled with heat as each refused to look away. Sybil broke the stare when a knock sounded on her screen door.

Calum nodded at her. "'Morning."

Sybil's eyes locked with Duncan's. "Come in, Calum. How nice to see you. We were just chatting about your investigative techniques."

"Always useful in a dangerous situation. I understand you're quite good, too," he stated without apology. Calum stepped into the kitchen, sniffed appreciatively and held out a basket of herb starts to her. Lemon balm and fennel added a bite to the sweet wood scents, tarragon and thyme. "Elspeth says to plant these on the shady side of the house."

"I hope they were obtained legally." Sybil bent to nuzzle the lemon balm scents, and found Duncan's stark desire when she looked up. "Thank you, Calum," she managed unsteadily, rocked by the uncertainty and the answering tinge within her. "How nice of you to bring them. I'll call Elspeth later."

"I like chocolate cake," he returned, eyeing Duncan, who was staring at Sybil through narrowed lids. "Birk said you had dibs, older brother. From the look of things, you're not doing too well."

"What is this, a party? I don't suppose you would leave," Duncan said softly.

Despite Duncan's ill mood, Sybil wondered how it would have been to grow up in this close-knit family.

"No. I can't leave. Sybil wants to feed me." Calum sprawled in a chair and winked at Sybil. The second Tallchief son, he had fought Duncan's bullying the longest. "I want my slice of cake."

Sybil tried to muffle the laughter bubbling out of her as Calum innocently met Duncan's dark stare.

The screen door banged again and Emily launched herself into Duncan's arms. He picked her up off the floor and grinned at her, his dark mood quickly past.

"I missed you," Emily said, giggling as he tossed her once in the air and placed her on her feet. She patted his stubble-covered jaw playfully and Duncan nipped at her fingers, causing her to laugh again. "You don't look like what Mom said—a desperado. You look like a movie star. Sort of cute."

She smoothed the hair flowing into his collar. "And shaggy."

"Desperado?" Duncan lifted an eyebrow at Sybil. "Is that why women throw themselves at me? I thought it was for my sweet nature."

Calum hooted. Duncan tugged her ponytail and Emily beamed. "I missed you. I told Mom every day that I wish I had a dad like you—"

"Emily!" Sybil shook her head slightly and Emily blushed, gazing up at Duncan with adoring eyes.

"He's not that great," Calum muttered, and held out his arm to flex a muscle and study it theatrically. "He's old and worn-out. I've got more desperado appeal. I'm great uncle material."

Duncan's disbelieving snort caused Emily to giggle again. She hugged him and Sybil remembered how badly she wanted her daughter to have a father. Frank hadn't cared and Emily had remained unshared. Emily had been Sybil's alone for so long that the thought was frightening—

Just as frightening as the light touch of Duncan's finger as it trailed down her cheek.

His eyes said there would be another time…when they were alone, and then he was gone, with Emily skipping after him. The screen door crashed and Sybil pressed her lips together. Wherever Duncan passed there was noise and storms and motion. Even when he was still, energy snapped around him. A flash of steel-gray eyes, a movement of his hand, a tensing of his jaw—nothing about Duncan was calm. He strode rather than walked, a long-legged western man who always knew his path. She preferred quiet. And safety. Where he was concerned, Duncan offered none of that commodity to her.

Sybil crossed her arms over her chest and watched Duncan swing Emily up on his horse. He held the reins and began walking down the street with her. Emily trusted the brothers; they could lead her anywhere. For a moment, a sadness went zipping through Sybil. Her baby was no longer hers alone.

"That man…" she finally muttered, and turned to find Calum dipping his finger in the chocolate frosting.

He had such a guilty, boyish look when she caught him that Sybil couldn't help laughing. Apparently all the Tallchief men were rogues and full of themselves.

Three

——

Duncan stared at the neat handwriting on the new check in his hand. Every letter was slanted perfectly, the curves exactly riding the lines. Sybil was like that—exact, cool, remote, with a deep, carefully shielded stubborn streak.

Calum and Birk pulled their attention from Emily, who was earnestly trying to milk a cow in the barn. After two weeks in Amen Flats, Emily had blossomed. She looked like any other country girl her age as she scolded the cow for not holding still. It was Calum's day to play uncle and he was looking forward to another slice of Sybil's cake before he left for Denver. He peered at the check and frowned. "Taking money from Sybil?"

Duncan folded the check and tucked it into his pocket. "I am trying to be sweet."

Birk grinned. "Right. Syb is the first female not to fall for your brooding 'desperado' act. You'll have to dust off your manners to catch her."

"Lay off," Duncan returned easily. "Or I'll tell Elspeth that you'll wear a kilt if she'll make you one."

"Now, that's a serious threat," Birk stated. "She's been threatening us with that since . . . since we all decided we'd reclaim Una's dowry and Elspeth found notes on the plaid."

Emily stood up and grinned, lifting her bucket of milk. "What now?" she asked the brothers, beaming at them.

"We take it home to your mother," Duncan said.

"Really? We can have it?"

Duncan winked, cherishing the thought of Sybil's carefully concealed temper rising to the bait. "She can make me pudding and chocolate-buttermilk cake and butter for fresh-baked bread."

Birk stuck his finger in the cream-rich milk and sucked it. "Cow's milk. You're pitiful, older brother. I'd have brought chocolates and a good year of champagne."

"Or flowers with a good video movie. Maybe with take-out Chinese food," Calum added with a disgusted tone. "You're ruining our reputation, Duncan."

"Huh?" Emily asked, looking curiously at each one.

"Since he's old and rusty, I'll help older brother out. After this, he's on his own." Then Calum invited Emily to ride out into the pasture with him to see the horses.

Emily glanced back at Duncan and grinned.

Wrapped in her research, Sybil dismissed the light knock on the kitchen door. She continued working in her office, tracing the heritage of a San Francisco matron. Marcella Portway was determined to include Spanish royalty in her family tree. She wouldn't settle for less, and if royalty lurked in Marcella's blue blood, Sybil would find it. She'd worked from early morning on the project, not changing from her nightshirt. "Come in," Sybil called when another knock sounded.

"Honey, I'm in my office," she said, studying the file on her computer screen. "I'll be done in a minute."

A moment later, a teasing finger prowled up her nape and probed the loose knot of hair on top of her head. Sybil stiffened. She instantly recognized Duncan's scent and turned to him. "You should have knocked."

Dressed in a battered work shirt and worn jeans, he lifted an eyebrow, mocking her. "I did. Twice for good measure. Come riding with me."

She stared at him. Just like that. Duncan Tallchief entered her home, looked at her as though he knew something she didn't and asked her to go riding with him. Asked? Duncan Tallchief?

Sybil tried to keep her fingers steady as she tapped the keys, shutting down her research file to keep it from harm. The way Duncan made her feel, trembling and uncertain with a bit of temper tossed in, she didn't want to lose weeks of hard work. She jammed her glasses over her nose. "I'm busy, Duncan."

"You can't see any better close up with those." He plucked them from her and she refused to ask for their return. She would not ask anything of Duncan.

He looked around her office and picked up a picture of her holding Emily as a baby. "She's a terrific kid."

Sybil reached for the picture. She didn't want Duncan too near what was precious to her, though Emily clearly adored him. Duncan resisted her for a moment, then relented. His gaze slowly took in her nightshirt with the sunflower on her chest.

"Been working all day?"

She refused to answer him and wondered if her rapidly beating heart lifted the material over it.

Duncan surveyed her cold coffee and the portion of a bagel. "I'll feed you," he offered. "If you'll come with me."

"Bribery," she shot back, wondering where she could fly for cover. "You'd want to pick at my past—"

Duncan's eyes, the color of shaded steel, pinned her. "Did you love Frank? Ever?"

Sybil rose unsteadily. The dishes clattered as she collected them. She refused to run from him. From the look of him, he'd catch her easily. Duncan was unrelenting when he latched on to something he wanted. She'd seen that during Emily's rescue. He probably deserved answers about Frank. She'd give them to him and he'd be on his way. "I tried. I'd hoped to provide Emily with a balanced home. Now I know that sometimes a single parent is better than two."

"You've done well alone," he insisted, pushing her into corners she didn't like.

Sybil tried not to shiver. Duncan knew how to hunt inside people, trapping them. "Leave me alone. I don't like nosy people."

"Cowboys who swagger?" he offered, recalling her opinion of him. The muscle running from his cheek to his jaw momentarily contracted. He planted a big boot on the chair beside her, effectively blocking her escape.

Sybil saw his lips lower to hers slowly; the dishes left her hand. Duncan placed them on the counter and settled his hands on her waist.

"I brought you Emily's harvest—cow's milk."

Her thoughts weren't on her daughter as she asked, "Emily milked a cow?"

Duncan nuzzled her nose with his. He sniffed at her hair, shampooed when her eyes had gotten too tired and she'd needed a break. "She did and she's proud of it. I'd like to give her a calf, if you approve."

"We don't have a place to keep one and I..." His heat reached out to tangle her usually clear thinking—

Duncan kissed her cheek, rubbing it with his, the slight abrasion causing her fingers to curl at her thighs. "She can keep it at the ranch. She's safe here now, Sybil. Give her a chance to grow and spread her wings. Give yourself a chance."

Her bare feet were rooted to the sunlit, warmed rug, her body leaning toward his.

Duncan eased her hand upon his chest, spreading her fingers and stroking the back of her hand. His heart beat heavily beneath her palm and Sybil felt her knees weaken.

He drew her free hand to his lips, kissing the center and placing it over his heart. The light from the window ran across his lashes, tipping the black sheen with blue and creating shadows to soften his cheeks. Nothing could soften what she read in his eyes: the need of a man for a woman.

"Go get dressed and come with me. It's too pretty to stay inside."

Duncan looked dangerous, almost desperate, and she sensed the tension running through him. Why would he be restless or nervous?

In her lifetime, Sybil hadn't played hooky or games with too-dangerous men. "I've got work to do. I ... uh ... I'll pay you for the calf—"

The hand paused. "The calf is a gift. From me to Emily. Every child in the county will be entering the fair. I'd like to see Tallchief Cattle represented in the children's division."

"So you're giving her one for selfish, business and promotional reasons?" Sybil asked as his heartbeat quickened beneath her hand. She hadn't touched a man who was affected by her. The idea intrigued her. She moved her fingertips slightly and steel-hard muscle rippled beneath the cloth.

"I like her." His muscles leaped beneath her smoothing fingertips. "Come with me. Out into the sunlight."

Away from shadows and privacy and beds still rumpled.... He wanted more than to pry her from her work, Sybil realized. He wanted more....

Her fingertips rustled the paper in his pocket and Duncan tensed. "It's your check, sweetheart. I can't be bought."

"I owe you for Emily's rescue," she persisted as his large hands circled and locked onto her waist.

Duncan watched her hair, a lock spilling down to her chest to cover the sunflower, russet on gold. He traced the lock, tugging it, until his touch circled her breast.

She stopped breathing, denying the need to arch up into his kiss, denying the fires flowing through her.

"You owe me nothing, but this...."

Duncan's whisper ensnared her with magic promises; his eyes were tender as his mouth found hers.

Her lids slowly closed as she gave herself to the taste of him. Peace. Quiet. Comfort. Those emotions swirled around her. Then she found the darker elements, the fire and the hunger, as Duncan wrapped his arms around her, gathering her closer to his hard body, his scents. He moved so gently that she thought she was floating....

Then he was lifting her, holding her against him, his mouth moving magically, sweetly, over hers.

Duncan's heat and trembling surprised Sybil as he nibbled at her lips, nudging them slightly open. She tasted his tongue as it flicked over her bottom lip, the tempting kisses at the corners of her mouth seducing her.

Why was she standing still? Why hadn't she leveled him to the floor? Where were all her hours of self-defense classes?

Wasted. Her mouth curved slightly beneath his light, teasing kisses. She was dreaming. Duncan would take a more than average amount of leveling.

He challenged her on another plane, taunting her with gentle, tormenting kisses. She'd never been played with or kissed like this: as though they had all the time in the world.

Sybil, fascinated by this strong man tempering his touch, moved closer, and his dark, hungry groan swept through her hair. He crushed the strands in his fingers, bringing them to his face.

She didn't understand the dark-red color moving up his tanned cheeks, or the trembling of his denim-covered thighs against her bare ones. . . .

"You're standing on my boots, sweetheart," Duncan murmured huskily against her hot cheek. "I've just come from work. They're not exactly clean. You might have a bit of dirt on you if you tangle with me. That and maybe sweat, too," he added, humor and something else lighting his eyes.

Sybil realized that she'd locked her arms around his shoulders, holding that safe, broad anchor while her hands caught his hair, keeping his mouth on hers.

His eyes were tender, watching the blush sweep through her. She realized that he had caressed the curve of her bottom luxuriously and that her breasts lay nestled against his chest. "Uh . . . I . . . you . . ." she began.

"Come with me."

Come with me. Just like that. He'd said that when he'd first come; now he demanded again. When he wanted something enough to hunt it, Duncan could be relentless. She refused to be his trophy—

Sybil shook her head and inched away, her body shaking. She realized unsteadily that she'd never had to step off a man's boot before. She clasped files to her chest, protecting herself against what he offered. What she'd never experienced. "You'd better go."

Duncan eased himself away from the wall, and with horror, Sybil realized that she had pressed him to it. He'd taken her weight upon him. He slowly pulled the check from his pocket, tore it and tossed it in her wastebasket.

"Duncan, I owe you. We can't leave it at that," she said shakily. She moved without ties of any kind except Emily.

His smile wasn't nice. "*That* hasn't got anything to do with *this*." Then he bent to kiss her before she could move away.

Sybil found herself staring, dry mouthed, at Duncan's backside as he walked out the door. The sound of her heartbeat covered the sound of the door closing quietly behind him.

Fifteen minutes later, Sybil dug her fingers into her arms and strode the length of the kitchen. Duncan was tormenting her. Elspeth said he was a champion tormentor once he'd decided upon it. Sybil shook her head. She'd actually stepped onto his boots to reach his mouth.

He could kiss the devil out of her and swagger away, could he?

She studied her trembling fingers, the ones that had locked into his straight, black, gleaming hair and the ones that had smoothed the hair on his chest. "Ahhh!" Sybil screamed quietly, releasing the tension riding her.

When she could, she'd pay him back—both for Emily's rescue and for tormenting her. Here she was, minding her own business, earning a living in her own house, and he'd pounced on her and demanded that she come with him. She promised herself that the next time they met she would be fully dressed, her defenses intact.

Then she saw the wildflower bouquet nestling near the gallon of rich milk layered with cream. Sybil stroked the delicate flowers, her anger toward Duncan flying away, out into the sunlight. She'd never had a wildflower bouquet—nor had she ever experienced the tempest that Duncan caused within her. She lifted the flowers to her face, the rich fragrances enfolding her. Duncan was too dangerous to ignore.... Every feminine instinct she possessed told her that he wanted her, that he'd inherited his chieftain ancestor's tendencies to claim the woman he wanted.

The flowers trembled around her face. *She was that woman.*

Emily came bursting into the kitchen, cuddling a kitten. "Can I have her, Mom? Can I? She's from Duncan's barn cat, but Birk said she'd do fine in town."

The way Emily held the kitten reminded Sybil of how Duncan had held her at first. As though afraid he'd frighten her....

"Birk said we should skim off the cream and put it in a fruit jar with a little salt. If I shake it, we can have butter. Real butter from a real cow that I milked. Can I have the kitten, can I, Mom?" Emily pleaded.

The phone rang and Sybil picked it up. Her mother was acting hurt. Memories came slashing back at Sybil, chilling her to the bone and made worse by the warmth of the Tallchief family. Emily slumped into a chair and fiddled with a flower while Sybil tried to deal pleasantly with her mother's usual unpleasant forays. Sybil noted the small ferns tucked into the bouquet. "Yes, it's a small, one-horse town. No, there is not an airport nearby and no, I am not moving back to Seattle soon."

She glanced at Emily and winked at her. "*Emily* is doing just fine. She's looking forward to public school this fall. She's going to get a kitten, a puppy, and she's raising a calf to show at the fair. Yes, business is good and I think we're getting along nicely."

Emily leaped to her feet and turned a circle, clapping her hands quietly.

Her mother's cutting words caused Sybil to frown. "My daughter is my business. You've made that quite clear enough. Take care of yourself. And Father.... Boarding school for Emily? No. Goodbye, Mother."

Emily hugged Sybil when she stood bracing her hands against the counter. Her parents weren't easy, hadn't been even before she'd told them of the rape and the coming baby. Sybil had always loved them, and the basic conflict was a war, hurting....

Because she had inherited her grandmother's share of family stock, she had threatened them to protect her child.

"It hurts, doesn't it, Mom?" Emily asked in a tone wise beyond her years. She'd understood from a young age that Sybil loved her desperately...and that her grandparents weren't warm family. The polite distance between mother and grandmother was obvious. Perhaps it hurt more than Sybil's own pain as a daughter. Sybil had gone to great lengths to reassure

Emily that she wanted her, that she wasn't the reason for the family dissension. It had existed long before Emily was born.

"Yes . . . it does hurt," Sybil admitted, and wondered who was becoming the nurturer and who was being tended.

Elspeth served tea. Evening shadows settled over her front porch as the two women watched Emily frolic with her new puppy. Sybil, dressed in a comfortable, light-gray cotton sweater and slacks, sipped an herbal tea while Elspeth continued, "The problem with growing up in a house filled with brothers and one rebel tomboy is that hot tea, served properly, isn't appreciated. I tried it once and my reward was hoots and slurps. When I cried, Duncan made everyone sit down and drink the stuff. Birk was certain he was drinking grass. I really enjoy having a proper pot of afternoon tea, nicely served . . . especially with you, Sybil."

"I enjoy your company, too." She'd lost a sister—Norma had always aligned herself to The Family's Reputation. Elspeth came close to being the warm sister missing in Sybil's life.

Elspeth lifted her eyebrows. "You've got Duncan in a snit, you know."

Surprised, Sybil turned to her. "What do you mean?"

"Women usually come clawing at his doorstep. He looms up there in his castle, the addition he built on to the old house. He plays big brother often enough. But as to what lies deep in his heart, he's kept to himself. And to us, his family. You're resisting his mysterious charm. My brothers aren't used to resistance. If you only knew the midnight calls I've gotten from girls wanting them. My brothers are too attractive and too cocky."

Since Sybil had moved to Amen Flats, she'd gotten a midnight call of the worst kind. With heavy breathing and coarse language, the unidentified man told her what explicit sexual acts he wanted from her. She'd handled threats before, in another time. Then there was Duncan, who was a threat to any woman wanting a measure of peace.

"Duncan is arrogant and rude and—" Sybil shot back, then relented, because she did like Elspeth and knew how much she loved her family. "He tore up my check for the rescue. I don't like owing anyone. Especially him."

"Yes, he would do that. They say we got our pride from our great-great-grandfather, a full chieftain. Una tamed him, of course. While he was swaggering and ordering his captive around, she snagged him well and good. They had a happy life, despite Una selling her dowry to keep the land safe. We've all sworn to recover pieces of it. Duncan came up with that idea just after our parents' funeral. We had regular family meetings to pick over Una's journals and pry out information about her losses."

Elspeth gracefully poured another cup of tea. "Later, Duncan told me how frightened he was—we were all frightened—and the quests were the only thing he could think of to prod us on. We lived through disasters with the lure of Una's dowry ahead of us. And the threat of separation behind us. We've recovered a few things, like the loom Tallchief built for Una, but so far not one of us has gotten what we set out to recover. I thought Calum would be the first. He likes tidy endings. But his career and marriage waylaid him, and then his wife died in an accident. They had just quarreled bitterly. He'll find Una's garnet ring soon, I'm certain."

"What was Duncan to recover?"

"A cradle. He tried, and then there was a kidnapping and his divorce, another kidnapping and then running the ranch. I believe he was deeply wounded when his ex-wife told him she didn't want Tallchief children. He'd wanted them so desperately until then. The cradle would be a painful reminder. He's put away dreams in his lifetime. I'm certain that raising us cost him dearly. But he didn't complain. Not once."

Elspeth studied the tea leaves in the bottom of her cup. "If Duncan wanted the cradle enough, he would have it. He's like that, getting what he goes after. My guess is he had plans for the cradle, and the scars went deep when his marriage failed. Sometimes the pieces never go back together again. I'd hate to see that in Duncan."

Elspeth's fingertip traced the flowers on the teacup. "Duncan says little about that time in his life. He's a survivor. We all are—he told me that when I thought I couldn't go on."

Pain quivered in the air between the two women as they shared a look, survivor to survivor. "Our parents would have been proud of the way he's built Tallchief Cattle. I remember listening to him and Birk and Calum working over bills and adding rodeo winnings they hadn't yet earned. They saved the serious discussions until they thought Fiona and I were asleep. They're like that. Protective and maddening."

Sybil thought of an eighteen-year-old boy, grieving for his parents and trying to hold his family together. Elspeth wiped a tear from her eye. "Those were tough times, but good ones, too. Duncan never let the rest of us know how frightened he was that he would fail. When his marriage shattered, he blamed himself. I didn't. Lauren wasn't the right woman for him. She never should have tried to sell Tallchief Mountain. Until then, she didn't really know Duncan."

"Tell me about the cradle. Where would I start looking?" Sybil didn't want to prowl through Duncan's marriage. The sudden, savage jealousy within her had shocked her. She forced it away.

Elspeth showed Sybil the drawings she'd made from Una's journals. "See? That's a Celtic design for good luck. Before he stopped hunting it, Duncan traced the cradle Tallchief carved to Chicago. He probably thinks the quests served their purpose, gluing us together, and we survived. So the actual object didn't really matter. It was the bond between us to get us through. Why are you interested?"

"I'd love to pay him back. Retrieving the cradle might be the way to do it. I've hunted for family treasures before. I usually don't like doing it because often the item is less than what was remembered. The client can be disappointed."

Elspeth petted the cat, which had just leaped up on her lap. "Duncan wouldn't be. He treasures everything he's given. He's got other ideas for you."

"I know. I don't share his plans. I'm not in the mood for an easy affair."

"Easy? With Duncan?" Elspeth lifted her eyebrows in disbelief, then sipped her tea. She thoughtfully traced the delicate rose pattern of her cup. "All the things we've pledged to find have legends attached to them. It's said that the woman who brings the cradle to a man of Fearghus blood will fill it with his babies.''

Sybil flushed at the quick memory of Duncan's hard body thrusting against hers. "Well. With it in his possession, he'll have a better chance of finding someone to produce his babies, won't he?" she asked a bit too tartly.

Elspeth laughed, a pleasant musical sound that blended with the tinkling wind chimes.

A hummingbird zipped by on its way to morning-glory flowers. Emily jumped onto the porch, cradling her barking puppy. "Mom, did you know that all the Tallchiefs cut their thumbs when they were kids? They made a blood promise to take care of one another."

Elspeth handed a cookie to the girl. "We got a tongue-lashing for it. Duncan paid the price because it was his idea. Rather, it might have been mine because I loved reading Una's stories and the blood-brother idea came from something my great-great-grandfather did. Duncan took my punishment," she added. "This is a recipe of my great-great-grandmother's. She said she trapped her husband with her baked goods. It's said that Tallchief men are suckers for a woman who can bake."

Emily giggled. "That's why Birk and Calum and Duncan keep dropping by. They sniff to see what Mom is baking. I think Calum likes her brownies better. He snuck two when she wasn't watching. But I think Duncan would rather have Mom's kisses. He looks at her the way Birk looks at her chocolate cake."

"Emily!" Sybil placed her teacup in its saucer before she spilled the tea. It was true, however. At any time she could sense Duncan looking at her, his eyes glittering. The taut set of his body told her things she didn't want to know. More than once, his hot stare had shot down, then up her body, leaving her trembling, while he continued any light conversation at hand.

Emily munched on her cookie and gave a bit of it to the puppy. "Calum and Birk say he can't run as fast as he used to. They tease about strange things...like Duncan forgetting how to plant the Tallchief kiss properly and net him a long, cool maverick and having to work on his pucker. But they really

love each other. It's warm around them, and Elspeth, too,''
Emily stated clinically, and Sybil mourned the coolness her
daughter had known. "They say Fiona would cause grown
men to shake. She's got a temper, but they say that if you're
in a snit, watch out. They think you're a witch. That you know
stuff from Tallchief's mother, a shaman, and stuff from Una's
mother, who was a seer.''

Elspeth's smile was smug. "I tell them that to keep them on
their toes. My brothers seem to have taken you into their confidence.''

"We're buddies. I even know that Calum has been married. He's what's called a 'widower.' I'm supposed to con-
sider them my uncles, and if any boys want to walk or talk with
me, the Black Knights want to know it immediately,'' Emily
continued.

"They're protective.'' Elspeth tossed the puppy a cookie
crumb. "Especially of girls and women. It was a hard cross to
bear when Fiona and I were growing up. Having three tall,
tough, grim brothers check out our dates and lay down rules
wasn't easy. They'd wait there on the porch when Fiona and I
came home with our dates. The three of them would stand,
legs apart and arms crossed, and glower at our dates.''

"They like me. I'm 'Little Sis.' Or they call me 'Princess.' '' Emily stated the fact proudly, as if she were wearing a
badge.

Sybil laughed outright. The image of the three Black Knights
led by Emily-Princess flew by her. "They've latched on to you
for certain.''

Emily beamed, her freckles shining on her pale skin. "I've
got a big family now, huh, Mom?''

Before Sybil could answer, Elspeth said, "I think you're just
the partner in crime that I need. I've been trying for years to
get my brothers to wear the family plaid—it's Una's Fearghus
design with a Tallchief stripe. The wool is from the descendants of sheep Una brought to Wyoming. Duncan retrieved
them. I've woven enough now that I could dress us all. I
haven't found a way to get my brothers to cooperate.''

"Tell me more about the cradle, Elspeth. I may be able to
help.''

"You'll have to ask Duncan. He managed to get a trail. The cradle seemed too personal with him and I've never interfered with his quest."

Duncan walked across the top of the building's beam, two stories high. The new roof on the shelter house would add space. In the heat of the day, he worked without a shirt. He needed the hard, physical labor to relieve the unexpected tension skimming through his body. He should have given Sybil the flowers; he should have conversed pleasantly. Instead he had frightened her.

It wasn't his fault. He'd always been a sucker for sunflowers and long-legged women with flame-colored hair and huge honey-soft eyes that a man could fall into. He glanced down just then and found Sybil gazing up at him, shading her eyes.

Against the lush alfalfa field behind the shelter, her cream-colored cotton sweater and slacks caused her to look very slender and feminine. Far too cool for the fire running beneath her lips.

Duncan wiped away a trail of sweat that had escaped the bandanna tied around his head. No woman should look so cool and inviting. Just the sight of her made him want to carry her away.

Or kiss her. He thought about her cool lips moving beneath his, thought about the fire simmering beneath—

Her eyes widened and slowly he realized the direction of her stare—straight to his bare chest. Her gaze shifted, tracing his shoulders, his chest and down his stomach.

His stomach lurched and Duncan sucked in air, surprised at the need surging through him.

Duncan realized he was flexing his arm, pounding the nail too deep. But from this height, he could see Sybil's eyes widen, her mouth part. He wanted to fascinate her, to rip away the cool facade and meet her as a man meets a woman. He'd have to walk carefully, Duncan thought grimly, placing the hammer aside.

On the ground, he poured a dipper of water over his head and shook his hair. "What do you want?" he asked rudely, aware that his sleepless nights, his restless emotions were pushing him.

"Out of your debt. I want to know what you know of the Fearghus cradle. I'm returning it to you and then—"

Duncan stepped closer. He had no intention of anyone entering his quest. But if talk of it gained him time with Sybil, he'd talk. "And then?"

Awareness leaped in her eyes and a quiet happiness flowed through him. She'd been as enthralled with the kiss as he had been, searching out the tender depths, tracing the hunger. He shrugged, pushing away his need to kiss her. Her eyes skimmed his shoulders, and pushing his case, Duncan flexed his arm. Sybil's eyes widened to satisfy him. So she was interested— "Since you've come to me, let me show you around."

A willowy woman with luminous brown eyes came to his side and Duncan nodded. "Wyonna, this is Sybil. She's Emily's mother."

Sybil forced herself not to look at Duncan, not to feel the brief rage surging through her. Obviously from the way Wyonna looked at Duncan, the tenderness in her expressive eyes, Duncan had one woman. Why did he want another?

"I'm glad to meet you," Sybil managed stiffly. Just managed, her fury whipping through her.

"Come with me," Duncan said curtly, taking her hand and tugging her along after him.

By the time Sybil had caught her breath, they were standing in a small, unfinished room and Duncan had her pressed against a wall, his hands on either side of her hair. He toyed with a strand while she fought her dark mood and the need to physically attack him. He knocked lightly on her head. "You're easy to read. Your eyes ignite like sunlight glinting off topaz. Now, what's going on in there?"

"You're having an affair with her and you kissed me." She exploded with the accusation, shoving both hands at his hard, bare stomach.

He blinked, not understanding. She shoved reality under his broken, arrogant nose. "You kissed me. Came into my home and kissed me. You touched me *and* you kissed me, Duncan."

He shook his head as if clearing it. "So? I like it. You come unglued magnificently. I have great expectations where you're concerned."

"Ohh!" Sybil ducked under his arm, only to have him grab her sweater from behind and draw her back to him.

"What's that supposed to mean?"

"Let me go. I was the karate class's top student." She forced her eyes away from his wide chest, from the sweat glistening on the hair running down the center of his stomach. His flat nipples gleamed and Sybil subdued the urge to trace and explore them.

Duncan's smile wasn't nice. He stood there, all dangerous male, gorgeous in his tanned skin and his rakish sweatband. His jaw clenched dangerously, the damp hair on his nape as untamed as the man. The color of night smoke, his eyes challenged her. "Try it. Take me down."

A gentleman would have apologized; Sybil didn't expect Duncan to do anything but stand there, challenging her.

She tried not to notice the pale strip of flesh beneath his navel, where his jeans waistband had slipped. She wanted to lick the drop of water trailing down his temple and nip the one on his bottom lip.

Sybil pushed back the curls that had escaped her tight chignon. Duncan could dishevel her too easily and she resented him. He could bring her down to his elemental level within seconds.

"I am not involved with Wyonna," he stated very carefully. He was unused to explaining his life, and his smoky eyes flickered. A hunter, he spoke too softly, wrapping his deep, husky tones around her with an intimacy like silk. "But it's nice to know you care. Next time bring lunch. Cook me something sweet and tasty, just like you. But with enough tart to make the taste exciting."

She recognized his challenge—since another woman wasn't occupying him, he wanted her in his bed. "You are positively beyond belief. If you think for one moment that I actually would wait on you, serve you— Take a flying leap, Duncan Tallchief."

Duncan shook his head, mocking her. He was playing with her. "Harsh words for a woman who came to see me."

Anger balled her fists. Sybil tried to remember that she had a reputation for being a cool, methodical, unemotional woman.

Duncan's fingers strolled around her lace collar. He studied the fragile cloth, tracing his finger to her throat. His fingertip meandered at her racing pulse. "Very prim and proper. Almost a virginal look."

She shifted slightly as he said, "If you take the day off and come riding with me, I'll tell you what I know of the cradle. But you won't find it. I lost the trail in Chicago."

"I am very good." She paused, shocked with her bold statement. His arrogance had washed off onto her.

Duncan bent to brush a devastating kiss across her lips. He nibbled her bottom lip before she could gasp and move away. For a big man, he moved very, very quickly, and she didn't trust him. Not for a moment. "We'll see. I've always wanted to taste 'good.'"

"Nothing can happen between us," she asserted shakily, drawing an unseen line between them. Duncan, clearly experienced with sensual play, couldn't possibly know how inexperienced she was with men. She wanted to keep it that way. Safe. Neat. Without Duncan smashing the reserve that had kept her safe. "I won't let it."

Duncan smoothed her hair, lifting the russet strands to the sunlight and studied the glistening shades. "There're two of us in this, sweetheart. Two. You and me. I think you know that our time is coming—"

Her eyes widened as she stepped back. She wasn't having any of what Duncan proposed. "No."

"Dress for riding a horse and wait for me if you want to know about the cradle. If you aren't a coward. Are you, sweetheart?" he taunted in a low, soft voice. It caused her to tremble.

At suppertime, Birk was treating Emily to a hamburger at the local hangout and Sybil sat alone at her kitchen table shredding wildflowers. Dressed in a bronze sweater and matching slacks, she dropped the petals into a plate and set about ripping apart another flower.

Duncan could see her through the screen door, and from the look on her face, he knew he was only a heartbeat behind the shredded wildflowers. She turned to his knock, and in that moment, he caught the blaze of her eyes—the woman who would like to stake him out on an anthill. She'd be worth it, all fire and shadows. In his mind, he glimpsed the image of the tigress stalking from the cool fern.

"Manners, Duncan. You need them. I've waited for hours. Riding horses at night can be dangerous," she informed him as she sailed past him to the waiting animals.

He watched the sway of her hips and found himself hardening, his boots riveted to the porch. He forced his legs to move, following her grimly.

Wyonna had been threatened and Duncan had returned the favor to Jack. He didn't want to tell Sybil how long he'd taken to preen and make himself acceptable to her. Nettled that she hadn't noticed, Duncan swung into his saddle and watched her struggle up into hers. The loose slacks tightened, defining the long length of her legs. She had a very nice backside, softened by the slight weight she had gained.

He locked his fist onto his saddle horn and wondered how the shape of her would feel beneath him.

Four

"This is what I wanted you to see," Duncan said, sliding from his horse. *What was he doing? He'd already been burned, and here he was, asking for a second helping. He wouldn't be good for her; she deserved a solid man, a gentle one with breeding who followed the rules. As a Tallchief, he made his own rules....*

Yet his gut instincts told him to capture her and make her his...his what?

Love as he'd known it could be sheer agony. He had no plan to fall beneath her spell. None at all.

The sun was setting on Tallchief Mountain and he'd brought her to the lake rippled by the mountain winds and glinting gold in the sunset.

Entranced by the red, jutting rocks and the stately timber studding the mountain, Sybil never noticed that Duncan had helped her from her horse. "It's beautiful," she whispered in an awed tone.

That's how he felt every time he stood there, wrapped in the scents of pine and fresh, clean sky. "Look—" He pointed to the deer grazing in the meadow studded with daisies. The

Scottish sheep peered at them, then returned to grazing, the lambs frisking with one another.

"You have no intention of giving me information about the cradle, do you? What do you want from me?"

Direct, to the point. He liked that. Duncan noted the lift of her head. With the dying sunlight tangling in her hair, the shadows kept her expression from him. He read the rigid stance of her body. She distrusted men, the set of her shoulders was defensive.

Her scent clung to the breeze . . . erotic, distinctly feminine and uniquely— Unique. Too fragile. Wounded. Hardened. Frightened. That was Sybil. He could hurt her too easily, with just a look, a word. Unused to the uncertainty within him, Duncan inhaled sharply, catching the scents of pine and earth and woman. He was driven to touch her one day, his basic instincts simmering each time he caught her fragrance. He pushed away his protective instincts concerning her. He wanted to touch her on a deeper level, the way a man touches a woman. There, deep inside her, held by the flowering bud, he'd know if she'd accept him on every level. He was torn between pulling her in his arms to console her and the heady need to kiss her.

More. To take her, to make her a part of him. To claim her. To sink so deeply within her softness that she would remember him forever and he would replace any man she'd known before—Duncan didn't want to think of Sybil's male relationships.

"I like your family, Duncan. But you've got to stop pushing me. You've got to stop giving people the wrong impression."

"Wrong impression?" He intended to ferret out her opinion of him.

She crossed her arms and looked out onto the lake. "You may like playing games with women. It isn't my intention to be a passing toy for you. I'd like what information you have on the cradle and then that will be it."

The finality in her tone cut him. He wasn't done with her, nor was she untouched by him.

"Now that we've had our ride—" She started toward the horses, dismissing him.

He caught her instantly, lifting her up into his arms. Sybil glared at him, refusing to push back her hair, which had begun spilling from its confinement. Disgusted with the tumbling russet curls, she ripped away the band holding them. He liked watching her unravel, fighting the temper nipping at her cool reserve.

"Put me down," she ordered, breathing hard.

He tossed her lightly, and watched her eyes flash with anger. "Can't."

"You're perverse. Tormenting. Disgusting. I dislike this physical—*primitive* showing of strength, for a better description. You know very well how I feel about you and yet you—"

"So you've fallen for my charms?" he offered.

"Why do you persist?" she asked harshly when she'd had time to circle that tidbit. "Don't you have other toys?"

"Sit with me and watch the sunset." He saw her eyes close as he planted a quick kiss on her nose.

They jerked open, lashing at him. "I've never been a fan of swashbucklers, Duncan. And you're one. A cross between boyish charm, a swaggering cowboy and—"

She found him studying her and pressed her lips together before going on. "You're a throwback, you know. All tall and proud and arrogant like your chieftain ancestor. You actually want me to continue owing you. I refuse. What is it with you, a power thing?"

He cuddled her closer, his thumb smoothing her thigh. Just holding her like this settled the deep ache within him. She'd laugh if she knew. Or think him mad. "You owe me nothing."

Sybil gazed at her hands, neatly folded in her lap. He wanted them on him, latched to his hair or floating lightly over him, taming the lonely darkness within him. Instead he carried her to his favorite spot and settled with her upon his lap.

"I'm not a child," she mumbled, sitting very straight. "And you're not that soft."

There in that hour with the red sunlight enfolding them, Duncan found his peace. Sybil gradually eased back, resting against him. He kissed her temple and nuzzled her hair, letting her softness, her scent soothe him. He feared she'd run from him; but she stayed.

She sighed once, caught by the beauty around them. "Duncan, this is beautiful."

"Aye," he whispered, wrapping the moment around him.

"Aye," she repeated more quietly, in a tone tinged with amusement. "'Aye, sir'—isn't that what you made Elspeth say as a child?"

He shrugged. "Arrogance and size won back then. She's been torturing me ever since."

Sybil turned to look up at him. "You still want life to fall your way. I can't afford your games, Duncan."

"Maybe it's not a game," he said lightly, testing. "I like you. We could be friends." Friendship wasn't what he wanted; she gave him peace and he wanted more.

"You wouldn't stop at that. I doubt that you ever stop until it suits you. You want too much. Find someone else."

"And let you off the hook?" he teased, rocking her. He moved her carefully so that she rested upon the sun-warmed flat rock. He read the set of her jaw and changed the subject. "We went skinny-dipping here as kids. I can almost hear Fiona's war whoop."

Sybil lay quietly, her eyes drifting over the lake, her mind flowing away from him.

But Duncan's mind wasn't on the past. It was on the woman in his arms. "Right is right," he said, more to himself than to her.

Her look—the dark, closed expression of a woman torn by pain—set him off. "I won't hurt you," he whispered against her lips, brushing them with his.

She lay so still he feared he frightened her. That the past had locked around her, freezing her, keeping her from him. "I've never been a physical person," she murmured, gazing out onto the black lake, with the gray sky hovering over the mountains. She shot him a rebellious look. "I'm not apologizing. Don't think you've lost it—whatever the Tallchief men are famed for. I have never been a sensual woman and you—you are too dynamic, you want too much."

He decided not to tell her that her fingertips, prowling across his chest, were raising his temperature. "We could be friends," he suggested again, and realized they already were.

She dismissed that with the curve of her lips. "Oil and water."

He kissed the soft hand that stroked his cheek. Sybil's eyes met his and clung. "You shaved."

"I'm trimming my desperado image." He smoothed the strands of her hair against the rock, the silk curling around his hand. He didn't want to harm her in any way; his beard would mar her fine skin. But there were other ways to harm this fragile woman—

"This is easy for you, isn't it?"

"No. I'm out of practice." He nipped her lips and heard her gasp.

She laughed then, the sound warming him. Her kiss, freely given, was worth waiting for. He held himself very still, braced against the tender, sweet tasting as she explored his lips. Sybil raised herself to her side, looking down at him. He waited, his heart racing. Would she fly away from him? Would the past grip her so painfully that the future had no chance?

She traced the shape of his lips with her fingertip and his body quaked. He pressed down the urge to wrap her closely against him. The nudge of her breast against his side caused him to groan slightly, he closed his eyes to treasure the moment. She traced his lashes and his ears. "Why me?"

Duncan lifted one eyelid to mock her. "Didn't your parents tell you about the birds and the bees?"

She flushed; he could feel her heat, even though the night was fully upon them. "Actually, no. I found out the essential details in an unpleasant way."

He damned himself for bringing her rape into the present. And he ached for the girl torn by pain, her parents' rejection. "It's not always like that."

"Like this?" she asked, bending to brush her lips over his.

"Very much like this."

She lifted to mock him with a smile. She'd seen the worst of men, the beast within them. "That's all you want? Just kisses?"

"Do you want me to lie?" he asked, smoothing her back. His tone was dry, laced with humor.

"You're a physical man, Duncan. You frighten me."

"No more than you frighten me." Duncan sucked in his breath as her hand hovered, then rested lightly upon his stomach. "You're a savage when you're aroused."

She glanced up at him, surprised. "No."

The night owl hooted and Duncan eased his hand into her hair, finding the shape of her head and bringing her down to him. "This time, don't hold your breath. I like the sweep of it across my cheek, warming me."

He folded her carefully closer, drowning in the scent of her, exotic and very fragile. She shivered and he forced his mouth away to ask, "Are you cold?"

"No." She squirmed a bit, getting comfortable. "You know that I'm lying on top of you? Doesn't that threaten something deep and masculine within you?"

He found honest interest beneath her teasing tone. "If you're so curious, we could try this in reverse," he offered lightly.

"No, I don't think so. You'd crush me." She lowered her head to his shoulder. "The lake is peaceful, when only a short time ago the wind was tossing the waves."

Crush her? He'd be so careful with her— Duncan rummaged through that thought. Sybil had no idea how light a big man could be, a caring man. He frowned slightly, sensing how virginal she was, though no longer a girl. He prayed that he could control himself when they made love...and they would. Every nerve in his body told him that they would taste each other.

"How long has it been since someone has held you? Cared for you?" He ached for her, wanted to take away the past. Yet he couldn't. All he could do was give her peace now. He hoped she'd come back for more, wounded kitten that she was.

She shook her head. "If you feel sorry for me now, I'll kill you. I don't want to talk about it. We should go."

Duncan bit her finger. "So you are a savage after all. I knew it the moment I saw you coming to rescue me."

"I would prefer to forget that momentary lapse. There you were, my only hope to save Emily, living the macho cowboy-chieftain image to the hilt. Though you wore jeans, I was certain a loincloth was under them and that any minute you'd dab war paint on your face. You were outnumbered and too high on the warpath to know it. What was I supposed to do?''

"Loincloths have their advantages." When his lips found the pulse in her throat, Sybil inhaled. Duncan's body arched slightly, nudging her softness intimately. His jeans were definitely too constricting. He agonized as Sybil's hips lowered delicately, finding him. Her expression told him she was curious, told him what he wanted to know. She trusted him enough to reveal this side of herself to him. He held very still as she lifted her hips slowly and lowered them again, her teeth biting her bottom lip as she concentrated on the tormenting movement.

In another minute, he'd grab those curved hips and— Duncan, though frustrated, caught the look of the sleeping tigress, newly awakened. "You can ignite now," he whispered, sliding his kiss lower.

"Mmm?"

"Ignite." Dressed in her nightshirt, Sybil punched her computer keys with a vengeance. She had lain upon Duncan's very prime, very hard body and kissed him desperately. She had rhythmically nudged his very full and hard masculinity and dampened at the contact. Little had kept her from exploring the amazing, heavy evidence of his desire.

He hadn't lifted a finger to stop her. She remembered the hard surge of his body to hers and the way she had melted instinctively, achingly, responding to him. He'd tethered her to his beautiful body with a mere touch of his lips.

Duncan was very experienced. He'd known how to draw out her reaction and he'd been successful. She had fitted her mouth to his and slid her tongue against his. He'd gently enticed her into his warmth, the rhythmic suckling echoed in the gentle arching of his long body. He'd tutored her until she'd matched his strokes— Sybil slapped the stack of research papers on her desk. "Ohhh!"

She'd never experienced an intimate, tender, playful kiss. She'd fallen like bricks—or flower petals struck by spring rain—under the light pressure of his mouth. He'd kept her on him, teasing her, enticing her, and she'd let him. When his hands had gently curved around her waist, following her hips to her bottom, she'd wanted— Sybil didn't know what she'd wanted, except those skillful large warm hands fitting to her, cupping her. Gently, so gently, his hand had curved lower, smoothing her intimately.

She was certain he could feel her damp warmth through her clothing. The butterfly-light caresses had tormented her until she'd pressed her hips against him, seeking more.... He'd murmured something about her scent—luscious and sweet, it told him of her heat; of how she waited, tight and shy and tender; of how he would press so deeply in her that their bodies would be like one. How her tender petals would enfold him— The husky, unsteady words had pleasured her—

Of course she wasn't waiting for Duncan Tallchief. Not one heartbeat.

The horror of what she had done, locking herself to him and taking, grinding her hips and breasts against him, had shocked her throughout the night. By four o'clock in the morning, she had to admit that Duncan had dropped the swashbuckler image and had been assaulted by her. Her breasts had ached painfully for his caress, for his mouth. Yet he had not— If he had wanted to prove that she had one molecule of primitive sexual needs, he'd succeeded.

Only his control had tempered her need to rip away his shirt and taste that beautiful chest he'd flaunted at the shelter.

She closed her lids and saw Duncan lying, rumpled and desirable, beneath her. The tenderness in his expression had frightened her worse than the trembling needs heating her.

"Kissing," she muttered now to her kitchen clock, then sipped fresh, hot coffee without tasting it. Five o'clock had not found her in a better mood. Duncan had not given her any information about the cradle. He was keeping that to himself and had lured her into kissing him. And flattening him on that sun-warmed stone. He'd been so noble to sacrifice himself, tethering her there with those devastatingly tender kisses.

"It's his fault." There he had lain, stretched out, keeping his hands to himself except for the exquisite stroking of her back. And the tormenting, light touches between her legs. A woman could get very warm next to Duncan.

"Oh, fine," she mumbled, prowling through a list of antique dealers in Chicago. She created labels for the dealers, and would send them a picture of the cradle. She'd pay him off and walk away.

Sybil gripped her arms across her aching chest. There was no reason she should be tempted by Duncan Tallchief. None at all. He was exactly what she did not want in her life—hard, arrogant, boyish at times . . . and devastating.

And tender. She'd have to watch out for Duncan's tenderness and his compassion. And his deep love of his family.

The composite man was too dangerous.

She glanced up at the pickup headlights, saw them die and hurled herself out of her chair. She met Duncan on the porch, the dawn outlining his tall, long-legged body. She'd know that walk anywhere, the broad-shouldered, confident, swaggering male, strolling into her world. He could take his confidence somewhere else. She wasn't buying. "Go away. Just go away and do not come back."

He looked up the steps to where she stood dressed in her long nightshirt. "You've got nice legs. Interesting kneecaps."

Kneecaps interesting? Sybil dealt with that tidbit while Duncan sniffed the early-morning air, tinged with the fragrance of herbs and freshly cut grass. His eyes locked on her.

"No kissing," Sybil stated unsteadily as he walked up the steps toward her.

Duncan tipped his western hat back on his head and locked his thumbs in his belt. The rakish cowboy stance weakened her slightly. She excused herself. She was only human. There he stood, rangy, tough and looking kissable. She'd had his temperature rising last night— The thought knocked her sideways; Duncan had trembled and heated. His deep, unsteady groan had been steeped in frustration.

She had actually...actually gotten to him. The evidence had pressed intimately against her lower body.

For a moment Sybil basked in the knowledge that as a woman she could tempt a highly desirable man. That insight shot to her senses, curling her toes.

"No kisses," she repeated, trying to deny the hunger within her.

"I'd settle for coffee."

His wistful expression rocked her. Early morning was never a good time for her, Sybil decided. She was too weak, her defenses low. She needed all her walls with Duncan. Every last one. "Okay, I'll give you coffee. Then you'll go— Why are you here this early?"

He followed her into the kitchen. Duncan's tone was too sexy as he drawled, "Couldn't sleep."

He took the cup of coffee and sniffed it appreciatively. Sybil jerked a raincoat from the rack and jammed her arms into it. She tied the sash firmly. Duncan's amused expression taunted her. She could have killed him. "I don't have a robe. I don't usually have visitors this early."

"Uh-huh." Duncan leaned against her kitchen counter as though the scene happened every day. "Lacey left a message on my machine last night. Jack Smith and his buddies know you're in town. You've bruised their feelings. They may want to return the favor."

Her hand trembled slightly. She fought the old fear and almost lost. She wouldn't let Duncan see her shadows, not now. Duncan carefully placed his coffee cup aside. "If you feel up to it, there are women here who need to talk with someone like you."

"Me?"

"You're a survivor. They need to see that. You're a strong woman, Sybil. No matter what happened before. You've built a life for you and your daughter."

"I... I'd rather not." Exposing herself could only bring more pain.

He nodded and flipped open the knot she had tied around her raincoat. "Think about it. And watch out for Jack."

Duncan's hands slid inside to rest on her waist. His thumbs stroked her stomach. "Be careful, Sybil. Or you'll find me glued to you for protection. I take up a lot of space and a certain lady recently told me that I'm not that sweet. You might not be up to the taming."

Entranced, she watched his expression change—darken as he drew her to him. "I'm not what you need."

She found her fingers had latched on to his western belt, anchoring him. He wasn't taking that hot, dark, dangerous look anywhere but in her kitchen. "I know."

He rubbed his cheek, freshly shaven, against hers and groaned. The deep, hot male sound hovered in the air and shot for her lower stomach, weakening her legs. "Lay off," he whispered rawly. "Stop looking at me like that."

Morning would be a wonderful time to make love.

Make love? Sybil had never indulged, had never been tempted— Duncan was easing her from the raincoat. It fell to the floor with her last thoughts to run....

He dropped kisses softly on her parted lips and her resistance wilted with each one. She leaned against him, sighed as his hands warmed her skin, sliding beneath the nightshirt. His touch eased upward toward her breasts, smoothed the sensitive outer perimeters. His thumbs stroked her nipples, just once, very lightly, and she tensed, jolted from his dreamy, sweet kisses.

When his hands slowly enclosed her breasts, gently holding them, Sybil barely breathed. She stood very still, the tender pressure making her want more.

Duncan eased her nightshirt away and she realized that he'd drawn her to a shadowy corner. Sybil crossed her arms, fearing what he would say as he looked at her.

Duncan's expression hardened. "You're a beautiful woman, sweetheart. Will this help?"

He moved too quickly, startling her. His mouth brushed her breast and her heart stopped. She knew she should move away, even as he took her breast into his mouth.

The heat and gentle suckling took her breath away. Her legs gave out and Duncan supported her, gently treasuring her breasts, the tip of one nipple, the underside, and then her other breast, already hardened, aching. She cried out then, latched her fingers in his hair and held him to her.

With an unsteady groan, Duncan trembled, his hand sliding downward to her stomach.

His hand curled around her softness, pressing gently. Something within Sybil waited, pleaded for his touch and tightened as his long fingers smoothed her.

When he touched her intimately, Sybil bolted, pushing him away. She covered herself with her hands, shaking with need.

Duncan loomed over her, the heat and tension pouring off him. She saw the hunger shimmer in his gray eyes, the hardening of his slightly swollen lips.

She'd nipped him.

Sybil blinked as horror spread into her. She'd tugged open his shirt. His stomach contracted sharply and released as if he'd been holding his breath too tightly.

She feared looking lower, yet could not help herself. Duncan's arousal thrust at his clothing and he made no move to shield it.

She waited for the fear to chill her, but it never came. Only the savage beating of her heart, the hunger of her body throbbing for his.

"Come here," Duncan said too quietly. "I won't hurt you."

Why did she trust him? Why did she need him? Sybil thought as she moved into the safe harbor of his arms. "Frank never touched me. I couldn't bear it," she found herself whispering desperately against his throat. "He changed immediately after the wedding."

"He's not here now." Duncan rocked her against him and Frank slunk back into the past. "You set me off. You're too sexy."

She let that soak in as she nestled against him. She shouldn't trust him, but she did. "No. I've never been that."

His lips curved against her temple. "No? Then why am I in this condition?"

She was horrified, her gaze drawn to the firm outline above his thighs. Her body ached, but she knew that a man— "Oh! Oh! I am so sorry."

Instinctively she reached out to soothe him, and Duncan tensed, edging back from her. "Don't. Just don't touch me. I...I could use a cup of hot coffee."

Looking devastating, his hair rumpled and his shirt open, exposing his chest, Duncan scowled down at her.

"Duncan. This is not my fault," she began, and took a step backward. He slowly drew his hands away from her body, closed his eyes and groaned.

"That is no way to leave a lady," Sybil stated unsteadily after Duncan shook his head as if to clear it and walked out the door, banging it behind him.

A nifty little thought zipped by her and she replayed it, savoring it. Duncan had been clearly aroused. *She* had ignited him. Sybil eased into her nightshirt; if Duncan wanted to play games, she just might challenge him.

She found herself humming.

"I have to check the hems," Elspeth stated coolly as she faced her three brothers. They weren't easy men to deal with alone; united they were almost a war. She'd fed them a huge meal, baked them their favorite apple dumplings soaked in buttery sauce, and yet they sprawled in her kitchen, defying her.

Calum leaned back against the counter, his glasses glinting at her like round mirrors. Just returned from a business trip, he'd stopped by Elspeth's to check on her before going to his contemporary home. Birk, fresh from a new battle with Lacey, had dived into Elspeth's beef-and-potatoes meal as though he hadn't eaten for a year. Duncan—looking as untamed as ever, his hair shaggy down to his collar—sat, boots propped on another chair, leveling a dark Tallchief frown at her.

She leveled one back, careless of her brothers' set expressions. "I cooked a meat-and-potato dinner, not my usual fare, dear brothers. I prefer pasta and salad. But oh, no. I'm only here to serve my family. I suggest you cooperate or our family dinners are going to have a very leafy, green look to them."

"Fodder," Birk said, disgusted by the thought of salad without a hefty beef menu.

"What's right is right," Elspeth stated airily as Calum began to clean away the table. "As the sister who bothers to sew on your missing buttons and make chicken soup for you when you have the sniffles, I demand that you submit."

"Submit," Duncan repeated, glowering at her. "She gets ornery when she uses that word."

"I never asked for your chicken soup when I had pneumonia," Birk mumbled.

Calum came through with a thought that jerked the brothers' heads to him. "Winds. Cold ones, right up our backsides. We'd have to sit with our legs crossed and check the weather report before going anywhere."

Elspeth was desperate. If she didn't corner them now, they'd get out of her clutches and be prepared for her next volley. She was circling her next attack, when Sybil knocked on the door and Emily called merrily, "Ho, Black Knights of the Tallchief clan!"

"Aye!" the three brothers' deep voices returned.

Birk opened the door for Sybil and Emily. With a gallant, courtly sweep of his hand across his stomach, he invited them into Elspeth's home.

Sybil handed Elspeth a freshly baked cherry pie sprinkled with sugar, and Calum zipped it to the table. "I'll just take that."

"Behave," Elspeth muttered, crossing her arms.

Birk was just slicing into the pie as if he hadn't eaten two apple dumplings. Elspeth's cool, crisp voice slashed across the room. "Cut that pie now and you'll never have another one of mine."

While Calum and Birk sulked, Duncan studied Sybil. She had a happy, secretive look about her. The cool, ferny green of her blouse and slacks set off her fair coloring; her hair gleamed like polished copper, in the knot at the back of her head. She would taste better than the apple dumplings and the cherry pie.

Sybil glanced at the Tallchief family, studying their expressions. "Did I interrupt?"

"Not a thing," Duncan murmured, enchanted by her quick blush and glance away from him. He nudged her shoe with his boot and those furious tigress eyes whipped back to him. He smiled and moved his lips in a kiss that the others missed.

Sybil ignited nicely, color rising in her cheeks.

"She wants us to wear kilts." Birk's tone labeled Elspeth's idea as something she'd pulled out of a child's toy box.

Calum made a restless move toward the pie and Elspeth tugged his ear. "Our tartan plaid. Pie after kilts."

"Once Elspeth makes up her mind, we're goners." Birk's stage whisper to Emily caused her to giggle.

"Emily, I would be so grateful if you help me with this . . . little matter of persuading my brothers to try on their kilts."

"Oh, fine. Women of all ages bonding, forming ranks," Calum muttered.

Duncan shrugged. The brothers had always stood together against Elspeth's feminine whims concerning them.... Except when she really needed them. Duncan did not see this as a dire time. "Looks like we're not buying, Elspeth."

Sybil smiled at Calum, and waded through an appeal to his logic. "Elspeth has worked so hard to duplicate the design—the sett—of the Fearghus tartan, adding the streak of Tallchief vermilion. She's spent hours studying the design alone, let alone all those hours at the loom and sewing."

Her eyes strolled down Birk's six-foot-three body. "I think you'd be marvelous in a kilt. Rugged, masculine, dashing . . ."

"He's got knobby knees. Football cleat scars all over them." Calum bent to sniff the cherry pie and dip his finger in it. "How do you know they'll fit?"

Elspeth eyed him. "I've seen enough of your backsides to know the width. You remember those shorts of yours I borrowed for a pattern? I adjusted from them."

Duncan and Birk glowered at Calum, the traitor. "That's low, Elspeth," he muttered.

Sybil began to cut the cherry pie and Duncan's heart stopped. The graceful flow of her pale fingers entranced him.

"I baked this for the celebration. Elspeth invited me to see the grand display of her brothers in their clan's first tartan. You'd be so handsome, Calum. Personally, I've always loved men in kilts. They seem so brave. Mmm . . . cherry pie with ice cream later. I can't wait to see you all decked out."

Duncan cherished the smile playing around the corner of her lips. Elspeth placed her hands on Emily's thin shoulders and bent to ask her, "What do you think, Emily? After all, you're the Black Knights' princess, aren't you? I'm sure they would like your opinion."

Emily played to the question, walking around each of the brothers and studying them. "I will have no one say that the Black Knights are cowards. Unless . . . they won't try on the kilts."

"Emily!" Betrayed by their princess, the three men roared in unison.

Duncan picked through the mutters and groans and Elspeth's ushering of her brothers to the living room, where she had hung the kilts. Sybil had just laughed. The sound was like a tinkling of a wind chime, or summer rain falling upon a still pond, a flute rippling through a sweet chorus.

He locked on to her hand and tugged her onto his lap. She glared at him, refusing to rise to his bait.

"I'm a desperate man. I'll wear that skirt for a dance." He brought her hand to his mouth and kissed her palm. "Is it a deal?"

"Ohh! You are so maddening. It's a kilt, not a skirt. She's worked so hard for this and you are all acting like—" Sybil inhaled unsteadily, obviously warring with her need to fight with him. She shook her head as if to clear it. "I didn't come here to bargain with you, Duncan. I came to work with Elspeth on the—"

She glanced toward the living room, where Birk had just hooted and Calum was mumbling darkly.

"Your turn, Birk. Step into the closet," Elspeth commanded firmly. "Lacey said you were a chicken-heart and that you'd never do it. I said you would."

"Oh, she said that, did she?" Birk muttered, and a door slammed as he stepped into the closet.

Emily peered around the corner, to find her mother sitting on Duncan's lap. "Your mother has agreed to go dancing with me if I try on Elspeth's nightmare," Duncan told her.

"Dancing? You said 'a dance,'" Sybil protested, sliding out of his lap and smoothing her hair.

Duncan stood and bent to kiss her nose, dodging her swat. "Technicalities."

Five

The three Tallchief brothers, dressed in tartan plaid and white dress shirts with ruffles, loomed in Elspeth's living room. The sashes draped over their shoulders broadened them even more, and their scowls filled the room with a dark, brooding aura. Elspeth smoothed and patted and adjusted the plaids and kilts as though she were lining up boys for church services. They crossed their arms and stood stoically, as if they'd been through this routine before—though never wearing kilts.

With the air of a sister, Elspeth bent to tug up Birk's white socks. He kept his eyes locked to the ceiling with an air of resignation as she said, "Hose and brogues. I'll have to work on that."

"Boots," he shot back, stormy eyes locking with placid ones.

"Mmm. We'll see." Elspeth knew her brothers well. She had to pick her wars and with whom. Given a chance, they'd join forces against her.

"Our sheep probably caught cold over this," Calum muttered.

Duncan, looking miffed, enchanted Sybil. After his exit from the closet, Birk and Calum had whistled and smirked.

"Don't let them go anywhere," Elspeth whispered to Sybil and Emily. She looked at the three, tall cowboys dressed in tartans and socks. "They're very good at leaping out of windows."

"I heard that," Calum muttered. "We're not going anywhere with our clothes locked in the closet, sister dear."

Elspeth raced up the stairs and returned a moment later wearing a matching outfit. "Oh, great. The unisex look," Birk groaned, and flopped into a chair.

"Sit with your knees together, dearie," Calum offered with a grin. "Better work on your tan. If the sun can get through the hair."

"Likewise," Birk shot back, coming to his feet.

Elspeth pivoted around her brothers, clearly happy. "Let's stand together. I want Sybil to see us all together, dressed for the first time in our family plaid. The Fearghus-Tallchief tartan."

She wrapped a length of the tartan around Emily's shoulders and secured it with a safety pin. "I thought we would design a crest for the broach. The Fergusson original badge was a small sunflower—Una thought the Fearghus family was related to them. Maybe ours could be a peace pipe with a feather crossing it. Or two sunflowers for Una and Tallchief. Or five feathers for the five of us. I rather like the five feathers. We'll see. For now, this will have to do."

"Gee...all dressed up and nowhere to go," Birk mumbled, picking at the plaid pleats covering his thighs.

"Wind. Straight up the backside." Calum pitched that volley at the Tallchiefs and it dropped to the floor like a fresh cowpile.

Ominous, dead silence lay over the room until Sybil decided to support Elspeth against her brothers, who were looking as receptive as a brick wall. They stood together and glowered at their sister, very much resembling their Sioux ancestor preparing for a warpath. She lifted the tartan plaid at Calum's chest. "Such lovely work, Elspeth. Every stripe is measured and repeated exactly right. The vermilion is perfect against the green and black. What shade of green is that?"

"I call it 'Dragon Green.' A little extra touch of goldenrod in the dye. I've changed the sett a bit, broadening the vermilion in lieu of dark red."

"Elspeth, this thing doesn't have a place for a belt." Calum hooked his thumbs into the kilt's waistband. "I will not—repeat, not—wear that hairy purse thing."

Elspeth waved her hand airily. "Details. It's called a 'sporran.' Stockings would set it off—knee-length hose...." She pressed her brooding brothers into line, stepped beside Duncan and said to Sybil, "Oh, I wish Fiona were here.... What do you think, Sybil?"

Sybil tapped her finger to her lips, admiring the fine display of tall, adorably nettled men in front of her. Clearly the brothers adored their sister, and Elspeth loved them, beaming up at them. Though Birk and Calum were gorgeous, Duncan's dark frustration intrigued her. In her lifetime, she hadn't indulged in revenge—other than Frank—but Duncan caused her to forget the past and the moment was too tempting. There he stood, all broad shoulders and narrow hips and long legs, dressed in tartan plaid and looking like a disgusted masculine bonbon. She tried for a serious expression and failed. "From loincloths to kilts.... You're beautiful, Duncan."

Staring coolly down at her from his lofty height, Duncan lifted a thick, sleek, black brow. "You'll pay for that, Sybil-belle."

She batted her lashes innocently. Teasing Duncan was a sport that she could feed upon nicely. "I will? Really? Tell me more."

Before she could move, Duncan hauled her to him, bent her over his arm and kissed her. Enclosed in his scents, the ruffled wall of his chest hard against her and his arms holding her firmly, Sybil gasped. Duncan instantly took his advantage, deepening the kiss. Before Sybil could jerk up her defenses, she dived into the kiss, fed upon it, searched for more. She found sunlight and flowers and heat so burning it swept to the very center of her. She was strong now, taking, giving, slanting her mouth against his, nipping his lips as hungrily as he tasted hers. The hot wind washed over her, melding his hard body to hers. The kilt, lighter and less confining than his jeans, allowed his desire to lurch and press heavily against her.

When her knees buckled, she found herself released too suddenly, Duncan's dark hungry stare locking onto her. "You're not up to it," he said finally, when all she could hear was the drumming of her heart.

To her satisfaction, Duncan wasn't unaffected; he was breathing deeply, dragging air into his lungs.

He lowered her toes to the floor; she'd thought she was floating. She realized then that his hair was rumpled by her grasping hands, that she had locked herself to him and had taken as much as he, draining and feeding what lay within her. Yet she couldn't let him leave it at that and foraged for a proper sword to his challenge. Duncan was a taker...if she let him reel her in.

The satisfied smirk riding his lips raised her thorns. Sybil shook loose of the fever gripping her. She had to keep the play even. "That's one," she said, stepping up to Birk. She'd never played a bold woman, but to shock Duncan, she would. He deserved a nip at his confidence. "For your bravery, Birk Tallchief—"

Birk's kiss was playful and light. Calum's was sweet and brotherly. They both winked at Duncan, who didn't change his grim expression.

Emily giggled. "That's the first time I've ever seen my mom give kisses like candy."

"I'll candy you," Duncan threatened with a grin, and tugged Emily to him for a kiss on her cheek. She beamed up at him, her eyes glowing.

Elspeth looped her arms through Duncan's and Birk's and Calum stepped behind her. There they stood, tall and fierce— the brothers proud of Elspeth's handicraft, her intelligence in creating the new Tallchief tartans. And she was proud of them. Together, they seemed to grow and luminate, overpowering Sybil with the love shared among them.

Duncan raised his hand and yelled, "Aye!"

"Aye!" returned the others, lifting their thumbs.

"One more time," Duncan ordered. "This time with Emily, our princess."

That "Aye!" went straight to Sybil's heart. Emily's "Aye!" trembled with joy; it spilled from her bright eyes and grin.

Sybil wrapped her arms around Emily and looked at the Tallchiefs. Tears she hadn't shed in a lifetime burned at her lids, emotion swirling around her. This was what a family was, a gentle circle of teasing and giving and love. They'd managed bad times and now as adults they stood just as close.

Sybil turned to Duncan. Rumpled and fierce, he glowered at her from his height. She noted his fists at his sides, and the first step he took toward her she knew he wanted to carry her out into the night. She'd give her heart then and she couldn't afford the loss. Not to Duncan Tallchief. He would want everything.

She met his wintry-gray eyes and caught the set of his mouth and jaw. He was angry now; his moods ran as fast and deep as the wind-tossed mountain lake, not suiting her. He bore rugged, untamed male edges with as much pride as the family tartan. He wasn't an easy man, and linking herself to him would be a disaster. Survivors avoided disasters—if they were smart—and that was exactly what she intended to do.

"Cherry pie on me," she offered lightly. She managed to walk stiffly to the kitchen without collapsing.

Last week, when they'd tried on the tartans, Duncan had caught the pain in Sybil's expression, the tears shimmering in her eyes, and ached for her. He stroked his jaw and listened to the coarse sound of his stubble meeting his calloused hand.

July hovered in the clover field, the bumblebees droning over the meadows. Tallchief Mountain caught the heat of the day quickly and just as quickly tossed it away into the night shadows. Cattle grazed in the fields leading up to the mountain and deer kept to the higher pastures. Duncan, freshly showered from chopping wood, allowed the night air to sweep over him.

He'd needed the exercise to ease the tight need Sybil had ignited. Duncan ran his hand across his chest, rubbing the hair. He wasn't a boy, allowing his body and moods to rule him; yet Sybil raised something dark and hot that cried out for her cool touch . . . and her heat.

The breeze causing his unopened shirt to flutter was scented with a coming storm, hot and furious, that would lash at the mountain. A softer scent, one bringing memories, settled in the air—his mother's scarlet climbing roses and an ache he didn't want to name. He preferred the safe reality of thunder and lightning, the fierce elements of wind and earth and sky, to the uncertain emotions running within him.

He'd forgotten his dreams and closed his heart in a closet. He pushed the cradle away from his mind; he didn't want to ache for children to fill his heart, his home.

Then there was the driving, fierce, elemental need of a man for a woman. A woman who suited him. More than once he'd found himself thinking of Sybil's soft breasts, the sweet sigh of release running through her, her hunger as she'd lain upon him—

Duncan's raw emotions caught at him, matching the still, heavy heat of the approaching summer storm. He'd been away for days. This time he'd found a runaway child, frightened of her parents and turning to a street gang for comfort. He'd circled the family and found an aunt with the backbone to take and protect the girl.

Sybil had enticed him away from the shadows, stirred the old dreams.

For her sake and her wounded past, he'd be very careful.

He reached for the telephone after the second ring, unwilling to stop prowling through his thoughts. Elspeth was worried about Sybil, who had just dropped Emily off for safekeeping. Elspeth had watched Sybil's car race toward Tallchief Mountain. "There's a storm brewing, Duncan. She has no idea of summer storms—the washouts or the trees that can fall when struck by lightning. Watch for her, will you? She was driving too fast, not like her at all."

Duncan caught the flash of headlamps in his windows, and from the darkened open door, he watched the car wind up the mountain toward the house. "I'll take care of your baby."

There was a pause, before Elspeth countered, "Don't use that sneer with me, Duncan Tallchief. You can be nasty tempered when you're prickly as a wounded bear. Sybil isn't in that stable a mood, either."

"I'm fairly quivering with fear," he drawled.

There was a fierce, angry pause before Elspeth shot a dose of the truth at him. "The two of you are a fiery mix and you know it. Take care of her."

Duncan hung up the phone and watched Sybil lurch her expensive car to a stop. She pushed free of it and went to snap open the trunk, fighting a bundle that appeared to be heavy. He lodged his shoulder against a post, tethering himself to the porch. Because if he caught Sybil in the night with her temper riding her, he couldn't trust himself. Elspeth had been right— they were a fiery mix.

"So, you've come after me." He shielded the lifting of his heart with a drawl as Sybil struggled up the porch steps, lugging a huge, paper-wrapped object. Her hair had escaped its moorings and moonlight caught the waves flowing down her business jacket to her slacks sheathing her long legs. Raindrops sparkled on her gray suit jacket, marring the perfect cloth.

"You could help me with this, Duncan. It's heavy," she snapped, and the raindrops glittered like sequins. Simmering in her temper and fresh from the night wind, Sybil looked as elemental as Duncan felt with the storm hovering around Tallchief Mountain.

Her stare locked onto him and the jolt hit Duncan like lightning. This was how he'd wanted her, the ice cracked.

"Ask nicely," he ordered, on edge with his emotions and the woman whom he wanted desperately. She had nerve turning up tonight of all nights, when his own storms threatened to shatter his control. Yet he took her burden and nodded toward the door, following her through it.

She stood in the dark shadows, and God, she was fierce, legs spread, the material taut across her thighs. Her arms were folded over her chest, her head held high. He couldn't resist nettling whatever control she might have. It wasn't fair for her to raise his temperature just with a look. He placed the heavy object on his scarred coffee table—the boards were from Una's first kitchen table.

He leaned back against the wall and watched her simmer, an entertainment he had learned to relish. "Are you going to explode?"

She took a full minute to draw herself together; he looked on, entranced. She pushed her hair back with both hands and he noted the expensive cut of her pristine, white blouse. A pearl button had come undone with her efforts. Rather than act the gentleman, he preferred to cherish the line of her breasts rising and falling sharply within the suit's jacket. He envied the bit of lace that bound them snugly away from him.

"You are just as beastly as Elspeth says you were as a child," she stated finally.

"Your friend Elspeth is a tattletale. She told me you were coming."

"Yes, that's like her. She's a caring person. She loves you and I don't know why." Sybil jerked off her coat and bent to tear away the wrappings of the bundle. Paper and cord flew everywhere.

Duncan enjoyed the passion of her movements. "Are you like this at Christmas, tearing through the gifts?"

She paused to glare at him. "You could have come to the car and helped me. This is heavy."

"I could have, but I really enjoyed the sight of you lugging something to me. I found myself wondering if you sweat...or if nothing ever warms or wrinkles you." He reached to trace a crease across her blouse, pressing the softness beneath. His fingertips lingered on the bit of lace exposed by the freed button. "Could it be a peacemaking gift?"

"Ha! Why in the world would I want to make peace with you?" she demanded as another length of wrapping paper flew his way.

"I'm sweet. Elspeth says so. A real charmer."

"Ha! I feel sorry for any woman near you, Duncan Tallchief. You make promises you don't keep and you—"

He caught her upper arm, whirling her against him. "Explain that."

Enfolded in his arms, Sybil struggled slightly. "Oh, fine," she muttered after blowing a strand of hair from her face. "Just what one could expect from you. Brute force."

He released her so quickly she leaned against the back of the sofa. "What do you mean?" he asked quietly, tethering his emotions.

She dashed the back of her hand against her eyes and tears shimmered in her eyes. "What do you mean?" he asked more softly, and watched her expression close.

Smoke and topaz, the color of their eyes, locked and held.

She shifted instantly, hurrying to drag the wood cradle from the last of the wrappings. "There. That is the Tallchief cradle. It's the one that Una's chieftain husband made for her dowry. She wouldn't marry him without it. The cradle held their five babies. Her husband had to learn to live an entirely new life, but he did. He learned how to farm and carve presents for her. He was shunned by white settlers and by his own people and Una salved him with a clan all their own. But he never looked back. Neither did she. They loved each other. I think he must have enjoyed nettling her and they fought horribly."

"Really?" Duncan asked without surprise. "The Tallchiefs were known for their passion and honor. So Elspeth has been spreading our family history before you," Duncan murmured, watching the silvery tears flow slowly down her cheeks.

He cursed silently; he'd wounded her.

She shook her head, pushed back her hair and tried to swallow her tears. Duncan eased her into his arms, stroked the back of her head and hoped she'd let him comfort her.

"What's this about? What promise did I make that I haven't kept?" he asked unevenly as Sybil clutched him, burrowing into the curve of his throat and shoulder. Whatever edge drove her, she clung to him, her fingers digging into him. Duncan fought the fear clawing at him—had she been hurt? Had Jack had his revenge while Duncan was away? Had Frank's tentacles reached from prison?

"You rat," she muttered, jerking herself away.

The fury within him settled; he enjoyed having her passion directed at him.

She pointed at the cradle. "My debt is paid to you. It's a lovely old thing. I found it in the basement of a woman who had just passed away. There's a little carved feather under the Celtic design. I suppose that is the mark of Tallchief. It's no wonder that Una mourned having to sell it."

Her fingers trembled, then drifted, lingering across the curved headboard of the cradle. "I'm tired. I've got to go home. Emily is at Elspeth's."

"It's too late to collect her now." *Stay where I can see you. Let me hold you.*

She wavered, wary of him. Moonlight slid into the house, wedging a silver square between them. Thunder rolled and a cloud covered the moon. Duncan heard his heart beat, his need to hold her warring with his need to kiss her as a man who needs the other part of him held close and tight. "Stay and tell me about the cradle."

"The woman who brings the cradle to a man of Fearghus blood will fill it with his babies...." Duncan reeled with the legend, the thought that Sybil could take him within her and create a life—

Too late. He'd given up long ago, his dreams shattered. Yet his pulses hummed with the urge to make love to her. His instincts told him that one taste wouldn't be enough.

"I detest owing anyone, anything, especially someone as arrogant as you. Even now, when I've gone to all that work to ferret out something you should have already found easily, you *demand* that I stay. *Demand*, Duncan. I'm not one of your siblings to be ordered around. I doubt that there is a 'please' in you."

Duncan found himself smiling. Sybil wasn't giving an inch. He touched her nose and she eased back a step. He took another toward her. "I'm despicable, of course."

"True."

Before she could move toward the door, leaving him alone, Duncan lit an old kerosene lamp. The light spread over Sybil's skin like honey. She tasted like that beneath his mouth, like warm, flowing honey. "Storm coming. Sometimes it knocks out the electricity. Will you...please look at the cradle with me?" Because of her accusation, he was very careful in phrasing the question.

She'd foraged and harvested for him, lugged and struggled and brought him the cradle. Unused to having others take care of his needs, Duncan weighed the thought. A gift from Sybil was worth the wait; she had pleased something dark and just as fierce as his great-great-grandfather's pride. She had brought the cradle to him, rather than let another bring it for her. Her passion to rid herself of him was too contradictory to be true. Duncan salved himself with the thought and prayed she'd linger close to him.

He placed the lamp on the coffee table that had also been Una's. The cradle's rich, old wood glowed in the soft light and he crouched beside it. It was almost a yard long, but light enough for a woman to carry. Tallchief had taken great care to keep the wood thin, yet sturdy. Duncan ran his fingers across the smooth wild cherry wood, tracing the intertwined Celtic design on the headboard. The arced bottom allowed for rocking. "The Tallchief cradle," he murmured.

Sybil couldn't know how fiercely his emotions caught him—a woman of passion sharing his Tallchief heritage. His woman. The primitive thought struck him, winded him.

She touched the tiny, aged carvings running down the sides of the cradle. "There's the intricate Celtic circle. . . . The cradle is carved from a solid piece of wood. If you clean it properly, you'll probably find good-luck symbols."

The images depicted a warrior on a horse, claiming a woman who fought him; the tepee and then the five babies, carved at each birth. A man and a woman stood together, a happy marriage. Duncan traced her finger, then slid to the circle of tiny marks. "Teething babies."

She smiled tenderly in the lamplight and circled the marks with her fingertip, which lay next to his on the gleaming wood. Duncan's emotions shifted as her low, husky voice curled around him. "Mmm. Probably a Tallchief brother or a sister playing on the floor, peering at the new baby in the cradle."

"Probably." Did she know how she lightened the shadows within him?

"It couldn't have been easy—Tallchief and Una coming from different worlds and loving each other." Sybil's tone held reverence and disbelief that matched his own feelings.

Lightning flashed outside, violence striking the tentative sharing between them and breaking the mood. Sybil gently moved her hand away. "I have to go."

"What promise did I make that I didn't keep?" he asked, watching her. Her lashes fluttered and she looked away. "I'd rather forget I said anything of the kind."

He traced the carved symbols and prayed she'd believe him. "I always keep my promises, Sybil. Always."

Clearly she gnawed on a private bone that he had picked. "Yes, well. I've got to go," she stated briskly, rising to her feet.

He rose slowly. "I've hurt you and I don't know how."

Her tone sliced him, as brittle as glass shards. "Think again. I don't wound easily. Not anymore."

"Then why did you cry?"

"Duncan..."

Her unsteady whisper curled around him; he clung to the notion that it held longing, that she'd come to him...for him.

She looked down at the glass lamp, blue with age. "Is it a family heirloom, too?"

"Changing the subject?" He kissed her cheek and breathed in her fresh, feminine scent, finding it akin to his mother's roses.

"I love heirlooms, especially those that are cherished and have stories behind them."

"Una thought her heart would break when the things were sold to keep their land. I can understand. No doubt her husband ached just as much, his pride nicked."

Sybil smiled, her hand drifting back to the old cradle. "Probably. He made more cradles, you know, and got a good price for them. But this is the one, the one with the Sioux symbols, that held their children."

"You've been reading Una's journals, too." It pleased him that she wanted to know more about the Tallchiefs than what she'd learned to recover the cradle.

"Theirs is a love story, a romance that will endure forever. A fairy tale, really."

"Don't you believe what she wrote?" Duncan barely breathed.

"A woman in love writes with her heart."

"She was in love with him until death. And he with her. He adored her."

"You would take up his side. Tallchief captured an indentured bondwoman who was deserted by the people holding her papers. He took advantage of her, Duncan. He ran her down and jerked her up on his horse and made her his woman. She had little choice but to survive."

He shrugged. "True. And he had the devil to pay for capturing her. He had a few scars from it. She had very sharp teeth and dumped food over his head when he got too arrogant. In the end, she got what she wanted, a proper wedding and a well-trained groom."

Sybil closed her eyes and shook her head. "Men. I say she had the worst of it with your great-great-grandfather. You're probably just like him—cocky, arrogant, showing off—"

If her glance hadn't locked to his bare chest, Duncan might have let her go. Might have.

He found her face with his hands, cupped it, treasured the delicate bones and smooth skin. He took her startled gasp into his mouth and tasted the moist texture of her lips, once . . . twice. . . .

"Duncan . . ." His name was a spell, coming soft and sweet to snare him.

Her lashes feathered against his cheek, her mouth slanted, moved curiously against his, tasting. . . .

Duncan responded instinctively, sweeping her up against his chest and carrying her up the stairs to his bedroom. Lightning flashed beyond the window and thunder rattled the panes. The sound was no more than his heart as he lay her down on the rumpled sheets.

"Thank you for the cradle." Duncan opened the buttons to her blouse, one by one. He caressed her skin with his fingertips and found her arching up to him, all silk and heat and softness. Her scent swirled around him, a deeper, feminine fragrance beckoning to him.

The bit of lace covering her breasts floated from his hand. Her breast was so soft, so sweet to hold, her heart racing in his hand. Her hips moved restlessly and Duncan slid his fingers beneath her waistband to where she was moist and warm and fragrant. Her slacks came away easily; long, smooth legs freed to his touch.

She continued kissing him, moving like the wind, the warm ebb and flow of silk beneath his hand. He traced her hips, curving his hand lightly over them to edge away the last scrap of lace.

The wind crashed open a window shutter and Sybil's eyes filled her pale face. Her hair tossed around them, twining across his head and drawing him closer to her. Duncan carefully lowered himself to her, easing away his shirt.

Did she know that her fingers dug into his shoulders? Did she know how sweet she was, trembling beneath him, a mixture of heat and fear?

"You're...very warm...hot, in fact," Sybil whispered, then bit her lips and shivered.

"Are you cold?" The wind filled the room, elemental and fierce as his need for her.

She laughed unsteadily. "Hardly.... You've got the longest lashes."

He fluttered them against her throat and nipped her ear. He found the tender whorls of her ear and traced them with his tongue. Sybil went rigid, shivering in his arms. "I've got to go."

Duncan forced himself to lie still, his body raging with the need to fill hers— "Yes, you should. That, or stay the night. Because once we've begun, once I've tasted you, the ending will take forever."

Sybil scrambled into her clothing, forgetting the bits of lace on the floor. She was gone then, running from him into the night. He watched her car lunge into life and soar down the curving mountain road. He picked up the telephone and prayed that Elspeth could be reached.

She sounded sleepy and then worried. "Yes, I'll watch for her. Right. I'll allow for the storm. I'll call you back if she doesn't drive by here in forty minutes."

Without her glasses, Sybil fought to see the road; she'd forgotten them at Duncan's house. The rain slashed across the car's windshield, the wipers ineffective. The wind whipped the trees and small branches, and pine needles caught in the wipers. Sybil pulled over to one side and leaned her forehead against the wheel. She shook, fighting the violence of the storm beyond the car and the shattering need within her body.

She was furious. With herself and with Duncan.

What was she doing? Battling a war by herself? Duncan was responsible for her undoing and here she was handling the matter by herself.

"Marcella, I am truly sorry that I left your Spanish gene in the lurch. That your claim to royalty had to wait while I freed myself from one Duncan Tallchief. I promise I'll find your royal gene and document it thoroughly. But right now, I have to hold my own." Sybil jammed the car into reverse, backed into a turnaround and soared toward Duncan's lair. She threw open her car door and ignored the rain pounding at her.

Duncan swooped her up in his arms. He ran with her through the gray sheet of rain. She was out of breath as he carried her into the house and kicked the door shut behind them.

"So you're back," he said, none too sweetly as she struggled out of his arms. He shook his head and the water sprayed around him. "You packed up and left and now you're back."

"Everything is black and white with you, isn't it? What do you mean, 'once you've tasted me'? That statement is so typically you—one hundred percent male arrogance."

"Okay. You could taste me."

"In a pig's eye." She caught his stare, which was locked to her breasts. The rain had soaked through her blouse, plastering it to her skin, her bra— "Where are my underclothes, Duncan?" she demanded, furious that he had possession of something so intimate.

"Those bits of fascinating lace?" he drawled, and sent her over the edge.

Her body should have been chilled; it wasn't. Every fiber flamed with the need to launch herself at him. "Never pick me up again," she finally managed, out of breath again.

"No? That sounds like a threat."

"You're oversized, Duncan Tallchief. And arrogant. And..." She felt herself warming to it now, the need to level him. "And what right do you have, hiding up here, keeping your secrets while rummaging through mine?"

He shifted slightly, but she caught the tension humming through him, a panther about to spring. Good. She'd snagged his confidence and she planned to peel back his edges. He'd taunted her and this was the price. "You know everything about me, Duncan. Everything. And yet, you keep your secrets to yourself."

"Like . . . ?" he prodded.

His easy stance as he leaned a naked shoulder against a wall and crossed his arms over that magnificent, broad chest didn't distract her. Almost didn't. She took a second look at the rain clinging to the hair on his chest and trailing down his tanned, gleaming skin to his opened jeans waistband. It sagged slightly as he bent to whip off his muddied socks. Then straightened. Without thinking, Sybil snapped closed his jeans waistband.

Duncan's smile was not nice. "Are you getting on with whatever snit you're building to explode or...?"

"I will not have sex with you, Duncan. You're out for notches on your bedpost and you've got women waiting for you when you finally do decide to... to fulfill your needs. Count me out." She flung out a hand in a gesture of frustration, then jammed her fingers into her wet hair, pushing it back. "It's your fault Marcella doesn't have her Spanish gene and my clients are clamoring for results. And your fault that I'm soaked. You just took off for a few days, just like that, without a word. You come, you go and suddenly here you are. I like a planned schedule. All the pieces in place. You have no rules but your own," she finished as she ran out of breath.

He reached to brush away the wet hair clinging to her cheek. She fought the draw of his tender expression. "Where were you?" she demanded finally, and hated herself for caring.

"Denver. How did you get the cradle?" A question for a question, no quarter given.

"I went after it. It was lying under years of dust in a Chicago matron's basement. I will ask the questions here."

"What did you pay for it? I'll write you a check."

"Ohh! I'm paying you back, you jerk. I hired you to rescue Emily, and you did. Why were you in Denver?"

She held her breath. She shouldn't be interested in what he did. Shouldn't. Her fingers curled into a fist. If Duncan had been with another woman... held another woman... She fought the pain surging through her, tearing her heart. She stood her ground, calling him out. Would he care enough to explain?

"Someone needed me. A runaway girl."

Diverted from her tirade, Sybil hesitated. "Is she all right?"

"A bit shaken, but she'll be fine."

Sybil inhaled sharply, her nails biting her palms. Duncan infuriated her; he made her drag details from him like a miner digging for gold. "You could have told me, but you just left. Just like that, you jerk. You packed up and just left me without a word. I worried about you. You can't kiss a woman like that and then leave with no word, Duncan, no matter how important your mission. Those may be your rules, but they aren't mine." She rounded on him, jabbing a finger in his chest and allowing her hand to be captured and brought to his lips. She paused, distracted. "Since I'm behaving absolutely like a madwoman, I might as well get everything out."

She took a deep breath and crossed her arms, walking away from him to the fire. "You know what you're doing, Duncan. I don't. That seems a little unfair to me. But it seems like you. You just . . ." She struggled to define Duncan and her feelings about him. "You just swoop. I have the feeling that any minute, at any time, you'll pluck me up, toss me over your shoulder and make away with me. Somehow I think there's a step missing in that technique."

She swallowed and started walking back and forth in front of the fire. Periodically she leveled a stare at him. "I'm usually very cool and logical. How do you think I've survived? I don't just leap into emotion as though it were a heated, luscious swimming pool filled with jasmine petals and floating, perfumed candles. . . . Stay where you are. One kiss and I'll toss that cradle at you."

"May I sit down?" he asked too properly, and sprawled on the couch. "Keeping up with you could drive a man to his old age."

She closed her eyes against the beckoning of his body to hers, the magnificent line of angles and cords and textures and colors. "You have no idea how to behave. Not a clue. You've had your way far too long."

His smile mocked her. "With women, you mean?"

"What happened to you, Duncan?"

He ignored her question, and infuriated her more. "I'll tell you myself. There you were, an eighteen-year-old boy saddled with a houseful of younger children. What were your feelings? Did you know you're still hiding them? Do you know how maddening that is? It's like this wall." She slapped the dark, rich paneling. "Do you know anything at all about fair play?"

He rose slowly to his feet and stood legs apart, hands at his side. Clearly she had struck something sensitive within him.

"You give, but you don't know how to take. Isn't that it? You move by your rules.... Make a note, Duncan. I've been through a lifetime of overbearing parents. I'm not about to add one more. While I appreciate you and your family's warmth toward Emily, I am not entering a relationship in which I do not hold an equal vote."

"Are you finished?"

Duncan's dark look said she'd better think about winding up her tirade. He wasn't used to being told about his particular P's and Q's.

"Not by far." She wasn't quitting now, just when she'd nicked that fine veneer. "Back off."

His disbelieving snort set her off again. "Ohh!" Sybil pressed her finger against his chest, winding up for another round.

He watched her pale finger against his dark skin and hair, then lifted cool, gray eyes to hers. "Go along home, little girl," he murmured. "Come back to play when you've calmed down. Better yet, I'll drive you home. You're in no mood to be behind a wheel."

"Are you laying out the rules again and expecting me to follow them?" She floundered, and knew she was acting like an idiot. Duncan did that to her. She tossed all caution away and lifted her chin. "I've decided that . . ."

"That?" he prodded while she circled the wide abyss she had created. That Duncan Tallchief had pushed her into.

"I've decided that I am ready for a sexual relationship. Oh, not with you. But I'm certain there will be someone—"

Duncan jerked her to him, holding her tightly. His expression was the fiercest she'd ever seen. She reveled in the knowledge that she alone had reached inside him.

His voice was too soft when it finally came. "Try that game and you're in for it."

"Threats?" she asked again, this time sweetly. "You see, lover—"

Lover. The name suited Duncan. With a sense of the gambler she'd never been, Sybil decided to have her due and take her first walk on the wild side.

"Not yet. I am not yet your lover," he corrected between his teeth, his eyes flashing like steel at her.

"Hmm. You're very good pointing out technicalities, aren't you?" she returned thoughtfully, smoothing out the peaks his fingers had created in his black, glossy hair. She'd gotten to him quite nicely and she'd decided to run him down and have him...on her terms. "You know about my sexual life...there isn't one. There's never been one because I thought I was damaged. I was terrified whenever a man touched me. But I'm not anymore, apparently—since my underwear is in your possession. And you know everything about me, yet I don't know anything about you. Is that really fair, Duncan? I think I'd like to go home now. You may drive me if you like."

His eyebrows jammed together. "May?" he repeated, sturdy outrage rimming his tone. "There's more to this than—"

She looked into his eyes, meeting his frown with her own. "Than what? We're far from being friends, Duncan. You've written 'claimed' all over me. So far, I haven't had any say in our relationship. In a way, you remind me of Una's Tall-chief...an arrogant male who swaggers and thinks women will come running when he crooks his little finger.... Well, crook, Duncan-lover. Go ahead. See what it gets you."

Sybil paused, rummaged through her list of complaints and decided to settle for glaring up at him.

He slowly released her and stepped back as though uncertain of his control.

Pride, newly recognized, shot through her. She'd never taken off her gloves and gone toe-to-toe with anyone—except for her brief brawl at the tavern—also caused by Duncan—and later, the kneeing incident with Frank. She studied the new Sybil and reveled in the feeling of being alive. She felt glorious, in charge of herself and thoroughly empowered. She lifted her hair and let it spill slowly from her fingers.

Through narrowed lids, Duncan traced the fall, then let his eyes drop lower to her breasts, taut and tilted upward against the wet material. Desire shot through his eyes before he shielded his expression. Sybil reveled in his need, that she—cool, generic Sybil White—had pried him from his shadows. She lifted her chin. Duncan would have to hold his own with what he had released.

"It's not like that," he said very carefully, studying her.

"What is it, then?" she pressed, hoping for the world, the sunlight and the storms. Praying against odds that beneath Duncan's fierce scowl, she had touched the man. . . .

"It's like this. . . ."

His tender, seeking kiss almost melted her resistance. Almost.

When she forced herself away from what he offered—because she knew she'd only won half a prize—Sybil patted Duncan's rough, lean cheek. "Call me. We'll chat. Hmm. I'm feeling much calmer. It must have been the storm. I'm ready to drive home now."

Six

"In comparison to Birk, Calum and Duncan are pussycats. I'll take a dull, predictable man anytime. If I wanted one." Lacey MacCandliss plopped her heavy work boots on the tavern's table.

The middle of July lay hot and sultry outside Maddy's Hot Spot. Inside, air-conditioning hummed, blending with friendly conversation. Ladies' Night, Lacey's idea, included lemonade, nonalcoholic drinks for those who preferred them and draft beer at half price. The paintings of naked ladies were shrouded for the evening and the jukebox was dead. Maddy had plopped jars of flowers everywhere and had sprayed the smoky interior with air freshener. In honor of the ladies, Maddy wore a T-shirt with no holes and an elastic tuxedo bow tie. Patty Jo Black was playing the old piano, a mix of soft rock, rock-and-roll and country music. A farm wife with rusty tones dipped in rhythm and style belted out the tunes like a nightclub professional.

"Duncan is not predictable or a pussycat. One minute he's flashing this boyish charm with Emily. The next, especially with me, he's all caveman." Sybil traced her lemonade glass's rim and remembered how happy Emily was to go on the camp-out with Duncan. At thirteen, Emily was blossoming, and thrilled to be his helper with the younger children from the shelter. Her feet never left the ground, once her mother gave permission to go.

Emily was growing up and no longer hers alone. While she loved the thought of her daughter adapting to the small, busy community and friends she'd never had, the mother within Sybil ached. She mourned her baby growing up too quickly. Sybil ignored the prick of jealousy when she thought of how Emily had taken to Duncan, claiming him. Placing Duncan at a distance was not easy with Emily constantly spouting his name and his all-magnificent wonders.

Sybil had intimately experienced a bit of Duncan's magnif-icence.

Lacey glanced around the bar. "You've got him going and he's afraid he'll tumble off his shelf— If he does, he'll grab you and run."

"I do not—repeat, not—have Duncan going or falling any-where."

"Ha. Anyone can see it's a war between you two. Under all that warrior beef, he's delicate, you know. Treat him gently or you'll have to deal with me. I couldn't bear to see him go through that pain again...." Lacey scanned the room. "La-dies' Night was a great idea. Seemed only fair, since all the men hang out here."

Elspeth shook her head and her sleek, black hair gleamed in the light. "You were making a point with Birk. And you dragged me and every other woman who could manage to get away into it. Because I took your side about equality in Amen Flats, I have to come down here every Tuesday night...whether I have work to do or not. I'm doing a huge order of throws for a gift shop and here I am. With you."

"So? What's your point?" Lacey, petite with a mop of curly, black hair around her elfin face, didn't back down. She tapped her fingers to the music's beat and swayed her boy-ishly trim body.

"Thank you for helping card the wool, Lacey," Elspeth said very properly in a manner that Sybil recognized as dry hu-mor.

Dressed in a black "muscle" shirt with a Harley-Davidson logo and worn, paint-stained jeans, Lacey propped her beer mug on her flat stomach. She shoved her motorcycle helmet aside with a paint-splattered boot. "We should get a male stripper— And I would have done anything to see Birk in a skirt. It was worth every minute of those hours of carding all that wool. Sybil, how about a brewski?"

"Do not say the word 'skirt' around my brothers, dear Lacey, or..." Elspeth's tone implied dire threat.

Sybil decided that anyone in Lacey's near vicinity could do nothing but adore her. As graceful as a dancer and only five foot three, Lacey was in constant motion, tossing off energetic sparks to anyone around her. At any minute, Sybil expected Lacey to leap onto the tavern's table, dancing Cossack-style. She owned a small remodeling and construction business and the men working for her could barely keep up with her whirlwind pace.

"A brewski," Elspeth muttered delicately. "The last time you talked like that, Birk carried you out of here on his shoulder. You were sick everywhere."

Lacey leveled a look at Elspeth. "He's *your* brother. He challenged me to outdrink him. Anyone knows you don't carry a person with an upset stomach over rock-hard shoulders. Besides, that was years ago."

"So I'm responsible, right?" Elspeth shook her head. "It was only two years ago and you frightened Birk badly. You're almost family, Lacey. You should know when he's tormenting you."

Lacey frowned. "I've been putting up with him for years. Just because you Tallchiefs have one black sheep doesn't mean you're all bad."

Lacey looked at Sybil. "Duncan almost raised me. Tucked me into their brood when no one was watching. Matt and Pauline Tallchief were probably the only parents I ever knew. I sat at their table like one of their own." Her expression darkened with memories of the past. "Those were the only meals where I had enough to eat and there was enough love around the table to spare—even when they were arguing, if you can call it that. My earliest memories are of my parents brawling. Then at school, while I had my fights, no one messed with the Tallchief family. Duncan, Calum and okay...Birk, too, pulled me out of more scraps than you can imagine.''

"You and Fiona drew trouble like a magnet," Elspeth said with a grin, and hugged Lacey, who obviously enjoyed the gesture.

"We had our times," Lacey said smugly with an impish grin. "She wrote me. She's trying to jerk the rug out from under a crooked developer in Arizona."

Elspeth shook her head. "That's Fiona. If there's a cause, she'll go for it."

Sybil wished for a moment that she'd been as tough as Lacey, that she'd fought instead of endured. Duncan brought out thorns she hadn't realized she possessed.

"Duncan cut my thumb and his, too. Stuck me with his penknife after...well, after something unpleasant happened with my parents. He said I was to come to him or any of the Tallchiefs when I needed them—for anything. And I did. I knew someone cared for me. That I was part of a family. Pauline Tallchief was the sweetest woman I know and she never backed down from a fight. With the Tallchiefs around me, I survived. Just like you, Sybil White, Miss Long Cool One who has Duncan Tallchief on her mind."

"I do not."

"Shoot." Lacey's snort denied Sybil's claim. She leaned closer to Sybil, her gaze too sharp. "You found it, didn't you? Whatever Duncan is holding too close."

"What do you mean?" Elspeth asked sharply, sensitive to any problems within her well-tended brood.

Her expression serious, Lacey nodded to Sybil. "You have to be a hoarder to recognize another one. And Duncan has been hoarding since your parents passed away. Sybil has peeled back something in him that he's kept hidden and he doesn't like her prodding through his ashes. He's used to setting terms and having everyone follow them."

Elspeth frowned lightly. "He was shattered by our parents' deaths. And then his marriage."

Lacey's fine, black brows lifted. "He never cried or complained, Elspeth. He did what was expected of him. That left little time for understanding of himself. Then his brood flew the coop."

"He grieved. I'd find him staring off into space or at the graves. He looked so lonely."

"He's not like Calum or Birk. Calum is methodical and cool—ah, therefore Calum the cool, right? And Birk is disgusting—he actually salivates around women. But Duncan's still waters run deep and swift and this lady here has set him off. The air sizzles when he looks at her and she's like a high-strung filly around him. I saw it down at the center."

"Oh, good grief," Sybil muttered, and shook her head. "We're talking farm animals, right?"

"Okay, okay, so it's a dark and...hot night. But you've got him netted, Sybil. And he doesn't like you calling the terms," Lacey returned with a impish grin, and leaped to her feet. She arched and flexed gracefully, like a dancer before a performance. "Sitting isn't for me. I get restless. Tomorrow I start another remodeling project and the lady has already changed her mind five times about one wall. Since I snapped that contract from under Birk's nose with a low bid, I guess I'm doomed. How about line dancing a few?"

"Make 'em eat dirt." Lacey's order echoed in Sybil's ears as she bent, bottom in the air, placing her hands on Duncan's lawn. Duncan, in the same pose opposite Sybil, blocked everything from her vision. She tried not to look at his shoulders, flexing and gleaming and broad.

Emily played cheerleader on the sideline and children screamed for their parents.

Sybil hadn't played touch football before. Ever. Her self-protection classes had been her only athletic adventures. Lacey had been firm; she wasn't losing another year to Birk's team and with Sybil she believed she had a "killer edge."

The afternoon game preceded a bonfire wiener roast that evening, hosted by Duncan. It was his first party, Lacey had said, and he was showing off his fangs for Sybil. With Duncan distracted by "edge," Lacey felt the football game lay in her small fist.

The summer wind, scented of pines and sunshine, swept across the spacious lawn. Duncan faced Sybil. "You'll have to go some to catch me."

Sybil caught Duncan's smirk and instantly her competitive instincts lurched to life. "You think you'll win, don't you?"

"Always do." The boyish grin on a man wearing afternoon stubble could devastate Sleeping Beauty—while she was sleeping....

"Not this time, Mr. Tallchief. And don't wait for me to do any running after you." She tried not to glance at his shoulders, and failed. A muscle rippled and she almost jumped. Duncan flexed his arm again and she glared at him.

"What's the bet?" His glance settled on her lips, then rose to the neon-pink shorts covering her bottom, high in the air. "That's up too high. Good form, though."

Sybil wanted to take him to the ground and demolish him. Her family's admonition to "act like a lady" didn't apply with Duncan Tallchief. She flexed her muscles, loosening up. "Get ready to lose."

Lacey yelled impatiently, "Okay, okay. Cut the chatter. Birk, you are dead meat."

Sybil inhaled and watched Duncan's eyes cut down to her Harley-Davidson muscle shirt, a gift from Lacey. "If you please," she snapped at Duncan.

Sybil glanced down the line of opposing players. There was Calum on her team, bent to pass the ball through his legs to Lacey. Birk, facing Calum, had just blown a kiss to Lacey, and grinned when she ignited.

The five-man teams were balanced and Lacey was out for blood. In the huddle she had ordered, "Do what you have to do. Just be there when I toss the ball to you. They think I'll pass to Calum, but I won't." Lacey had wiped the sweat from her face and whispered to Sybil, "Tallchief men never hurt women. Fake pain, flutter your lashes, say something outrageous. Just get him off-balance. In games, Duncan is a wild card, not predictable at all. You just think you've got him pegged and he throws a curve. Toss something at him that will shake him."

She had glanced at Duncan. "He's got great eyes. Expressive, you know? Watch him. He's a pushover. I'm going right over the top of Calum—got that, Calum? Give me a lift, okay? Calculate the amount of thrust for around one hundred pounds. I can somersault over Birk before he knows what's happening.''

Calum had snorted. "You don't weigh a hundred soaking wet.''

"I make up for it." Lacey's eyes had darted to Sybil. "I'll act like I've twisted my ankle, and while their big, strong, slow male brains deal with that, I'll toss the ball to Sybil, who is just low-down nasty enough—no offense, Elspeth, but you don't have a mean bone in your body. When it comes to Duncan, Sybil is all thorns. I'm counting on you, Syb. *I want this game,*" she had demanded.

"Lacey is up to no good." Duncan, across from Sybil, frowned at Lacey. "She's got murder written on her face. She knows she hasn't a chance without Fiona.''

Sybil looked at the wide set of his shoulders and the teasing, you'll-never-win, arrogant gleam in his eyes and knew how Lacey felt. "Don't be so sure, big guy," Sybil murmured, and fluttered her lashes. She hiked up her bottom and his eyes jerked upward.

She hadn't done much smirking inwardly, but Duncan was definitely susceptible. Lacey was right.

Duncan blinked, then frowned. To add just the right touch, Sybil formed a kiss with her lips and blew it at him.

"I'm going to enjoy this," Duncan threatened warily.

"Try, why don't you?" Sybil asked, feeling very empowered as he struggled to get a fix on her behavior.

The count sounded, Calum passed the ball through his legs and tossed Lacey into the air. She somersaulted, stepped on Birk's back and came down like a feather. She hesitated, then let out a cry and began to fold slowly.

Instantly Birk and Duncan stopped—Duncan was standing, blocking Sybil's path. She dived around him and ran before Lacey tossed the ball. It landed just right; she tucked it to her body and leaped over the player Calum had just downed. Lacey was cheering wildly behind her—Birk was yelling for her to get off his back.

The goal tree was only yards from her, when Duncan scooped Sybil up, tossed her over his shoulder and ran into the woods with her.

Upside-down, Sybil dropped the ball and braced her hands on his waist. She yelled, actually forgot everything and cursed Duncan Tallchief into the earth.

"Our point, our point! We won!" Lacey yelled.

"My, my, Sybil-belle. Such language," he taunted before leaping into the air.

For a moment all Sybil saw was air and space and Duncan. The next moment she found that the water in Tallchief Lake was colder than it looked. She came gasping to the surface and met Duncan's boyish grin. In the next second, bodies hurtled through space and the air was filled with shouting and laughter. Birk surfaced near Duncan and pushed him under. Calum splashed Lacey, Wyonna and the rest.

Emily swam to her mother and snagged an arm around Duncan. "This is the most fun I've ever had. A family picnic. I always wondered what they were like."

Calum floated nearby. He methodically spurted water into the air, the exact amount every time.

Lacey was crowing that Duncan had carried the ball over the goal line and that her team had won. "You did it, Syb!"

Duncan's eyes cut to Sybil. "Did what?"

She fluttered her lashes innocently. "I have absolutely no idea what she means."

Duncan blew into the water and it splashed on her nose.

"You have a nasty tendency to swoop and carry me off, Duncan Tallchief. You're not a fair man at all."

"Sorry." His tone lacked sincerity. "When you're all heated up, I can't help myself."

Emily surfaced near Duncan and held on to his shoulder. "Mom? Are you swimming with your clothes on, too? Isn't this great?" Then she was gone, heading toward an inner tube in the lake.

"What if I decided to return the favor?" Getting Duncan under her fingertips enticed her. The lighthearted mood had shifted and Duncan was studying her closely. His thighs bumped hers gently as they treaded water, and his hands smoothed her bottom.

"I'll try to survive." He eased her closer, his bare thigh between hers, nudging her as he treaded water, supporting them both.

Birk and Lacey were racing to a floating log. Lacey beat Birk, but he leaped up onto the log and began rolling it. "I'm for that," Calum stated, beginning to swim toward the log.

"Mad at me?" Underwater, Duncan pulled Sybil even closer to him. She allowed her hands to rest on his shoulders.

She shot him a hot stare. "What do you think?"

"You might not want to know." He grinned wickedly and Sybil found herself feeling very young and certain. Duncan gently eased her hair away from her cheek and his look lingered and warmed her despite the cold water.

The rest of the evening passed in an outdoor barbecue and stories from the Tallchiefs' childhood. Sybil sat with Emily on a blanket and watched the fire toss sparks into the night sky. Legs crossed, Duncan sat beside her. He took up a huge portion of the blanket. He eyed her lazily. "You could toast a marshmallow for me."

Her snort sounded like Lacey's and surprised Sybil. She turned to the faces around the fire. Love circled the fire, the Tallchief family tethered by the past and the future. They'd included others in their love. Emily was tired, but she floated in happiness. Voices were hushed now, the children sleeping on the blankets close to their parents. It was a time Sybil would hug close to her. She found Duncan's large hand had claimed hers, and the gesture warmed her heart.

She forgot for a time that she didn't belong. The Tallchiefs loved and cherished each other. Sybil had never known that warmth, or how to nurture it. Compared to the Tallchiefs', her family traditions and relationships were that of icy stones. It would be dreaming to think that she would fit into this happiness, and more pain if she tried. She stroked Emily's head upon her lap and knew that she couldn't afford any of it.

Emily reached sleepily toward Duncan and his hand enfolded hers. "Thanks, Duncan. This is the best day I ever had."

"There'll be more, Princess." But his eyes were locked on Sybil's.

Then his kiss came softly to her lips. For that heartbeat, she gave herself to promises that could not be.

The first week of August lay hot over the fields, and the streets of Amen Flats baked in the sun. In the cool mornings,

Duncan chopped wood. The exercise trimmed the need steadily humming through his body—the need for Sybil. According to Emily, she'd flown to England to research a potter's mark on the bottom of porcelain vases. Her client wanted to collect the distinctive pottery; he believed that the royal family commissioning the work was an ancestor. Emily stayed with Elspeth, soaking up how to gather mosses and herbs at their peak. Beneath the shady trees in Elspeth's backyard, lengths of dyed wool hung on a huge rack. On her screened porch, bundles of drying herbs scented the air. Emily had a small loom of her own, next to Elspeth's huge, ancient one, which she believed was Una's.

Duncan watched them walk together in the meadow, a tall, willowy woman and the girl, each wearing long, cool shifts and tattered straw hats. Elspeth had her shadows—a baby who had never drawn breath. "I don't want to talk about it," she had said firmly. She'd been studying in Europe, and when she'd come back, Duncan knew she'd seen too much of life's darkness. She preferred her dyes and wools and her family, except for the rare business trips to various weavers' fairs or to city buyers.

Sybil. Cool. Elegant, with shadows running just as deep as Elspeth's. Duncan narrowed his eyes, refusing to admit he waited like a love-starved teenager for the sight of her.

At one o'clock in the morning, Sybil entered her darkened kitchen. The crates of pottery were being shipped to the client; Sybil was exhausted after hurrying to return to Emily. She rubbed her back, the long hours of work and travel weighting her muscles. She'd fall into bed and surprise Emily with her gift in the morning—

She caught a movement and Duncan's scent, then found his arms enclosing her. Her breasts collided with his chest; his shadow loomed over her, his body like a wall against hers. His hands splayed over her back to stroke her. *Were they trembling? Why?*

She should have shaken free—he held her loosely enough. Instead she arched into his warmth and strength, careless of her draining fatigue. *Duncan.*

She didn't wonder why or how he was there waiting for her. She just took, fitting herself to his length. *Duncan....*

His mouth moved hungrily upon hers at first, biting gently, brushing to her cheek, his arms lifting her higher. "I missed you," he whispered roughly against her cheek. "Too much, damn you."

Then he lowered her toes to the floor and pushed himself away. He thrust his hands in the back of his jeans pockets and glared at her. Dressed in a cotton, short-sleeved shirt and jeans, his hair mussed and at angles, Duncan fairly bristled. He jerked a hand from his pocket and rammed his fingers through his hair, leaving more peaks. His look said she was the cause of his bad mood.

The space between them filled with tension, Duncan's raw emotions almost tangible.

She clamped one hand to the kitchen counter and with the other straightened her steamed glasses. Duncan, in full force, had gone straight to her head, making her slightly dizzy. Or was it elation? Did he care so much? Could she believe it? He'd been worrying, had he?

"Did you get what you went after?" he demanded rawly, his eyes blazing in the shadows.

"I generally do." She was too glad to see him, shocking herself. She, who had kept the corners of her life cool and unattached. Yet here was Duncan and her challenge.

"Sorry about grabbing you."

The apology lacked sincerity. He was a taker. Perhaps she was, too. Perhaps. Sybil plowed through the past—years ago someone should have been waiting, concerned about her. No one had been there for her. Duncan would always be there for those who needed him.

But he had caught her when she was drained, her defenses down. Sybil placed her hand on his cheek, wondering how a man so fierce could be so caring.

"I've cooked dinner. Would you like me to heat it for you?"

Her body heated just looking at him. The room seemed to shrink, the air too light to breathe. His jean-covered thigh brushed up and down on the inside of her legs. "Tired?"

Not really. Not now, the voice inside her stated as every nerve in her body latched on to the way Duncan looked in-

tently at her. Like a hungry man who needed her desperately.
There was something else in his dark eyes, a challenge that set
her pulses racing.

His knee moved higher, and liquid warmth pulsed through
her. "More," she murmured across dry lips.

He lifted a mocking eyebrow. "Whatever do you mean, Ms.
White?"

"Do it," she commanded recklessly.

"This?"

Duncan unfastened her skirt and Sybil forced herself to
breathe. She'd forgotten to in the last heartbeats. The business skirt pooled to the floor, leaving her in panty hose. One
of Duncan's hands caressed her waist, while the other supported her head gently. This time his kiss was slow and filled
with enticing promises.

Sybil breathed roughly, her hands locked to his shoulders.
"Open your mouth," she whispered desperately as he removed her glasses.

"Mmm."

He didn't hurry, his firm mouth heating hers.

She bit him lightly. Someone had to take charge of her desperation and she decided that Duncan would linger too long.
Was she on a schedule, at the mercy of a stopwatch?

Yes. The ache within her budded and flowered and she almost wept for his touch. *And he was moving too darn slow.
Trust Duncan Tallchief to be obstinate at a time like this.*

"You're shaking. And so hot. So hot...." Duncan's warm
breath swept across her breasts, now covered only with lace.
She tried hard to think then and felt the jolt shoot through her
when his lips ran lightly over the tops of her breasts.

"Duncannnn...." She heard a desperate woman cry out
frantically.

His hand curved slowly, firmly, over her femininity, his fingertips pressing gently, enticing heat until it poured from her.
She shook so violently, clinging to him, aching—

Over the rapid beating of her heart, she barely heard the
tearing of her hose. His touch eased closer, deeper, and Sybil
gave herself to the rhythm, parting her lips for his kiss, feeding upon the fire flaming between them. Heat pulsed from
every taut nerve.

She cried out when his fingers entered her fully, an old terror pinning her heart. Then Duncan's scent, his heat, the sound of his breathing enfolded her safely. *Duncan... Duncan... Duncan....*

She could trust him, her body vibrating with the volcanic pulsing within her. She clung to him, flowed beneath the gentle directions of his hands and fought the building pressure rising within her.

His open mouth teased her skin; her throat; the rounded, aching tops of her breasts. Every molecule within Sybil waited to burst.... She couldn't...she couldn't— If he didn't—she didn't know what—but Duncan should. He should know what to do now when every nerve ached for— "Oh, Duncan..."

"What? What do you want?"

"You know. Of course you know—" she managed breathlessly.

"Maybe. Say it. Tell me what you want."

His breath washed hot and moist across her skin, edging lower to the very peak of her breast.

Caught on the very tip of her passion, Duncan's hands moving on her, within her, Sybil believed she would explode at any minute. She shook, digging her fingers into the anchor that was Duncan as the waves washed hotter, beating upon her.

When his lips tugged at her nipple, Sybil fought the terrifying excitement, the throbbing within her pouring out in stars against a red haze. She wilted slowly, magnificently, certain that Duncan would catch her.

He swept her up into his arms and brushed a kiss across her lips.

Because she felt young and light and carefree, Sybil smiled against his damp throat. Then she began to giggle and couldn't stop. "Sorry. Nervous reaction."

"You weren't nervous a second ago and this isn't a laughing matter. Where can I put you down?" Duncan's expression was tender, yet bemused, sheepish but endearing.

She struggled to soothe him. "Sorry. Bad timing."

Duncan snorted, appearing very attractive in his rumpled, male look. Feeling very powerful and womanly for the first time in her life—other than their skirmish on his bed—Sybil cuddled close to him. "This isn't fair at all. Rather one-sided."

"Don't I know it," he returned grimly. "I'm going now."

Sybil studied him, this man who treated her gently.

He was the only man to touch her so incredibly intimately, to melt the cold. Duncan Tallchief was distinctly uncomfortable and wanting to soar back to his shadowy lair. Too bad. He'd chosen the wrong lady for sympathy. He'd started something between them, and she wanted more of him. She wanted to study every nook and cranny of his intriguing male brain . . . his psyche and his very fit body. There were parts of him that had seemed huge. An exploration when she was rested could satisfy her curiosity. She was very curious about anything concerning Duncan.

Carrying her easily, Duncan moved restlessly, and an idea struck her with the impact of a brick wall. "Duncan. This must be painful for you."

He flushed and began moving slowly toward the bedroom. He looked distinctly uncomfortable. "Not really. Not now. I . . . ah . . . well. It's not painful anymore."

She studied his grim, determined expression. "You . . . ah . . . didn't . . . ah . . ."

His dark, accusing look told her everything. The thought went soaring to her head, making her dizzy. Duncan was not immune to her lovemaking. He had exploded, too. She was sexy and all woman, able to affect a man who evidently had vastly more experience than she. She pushed his past experiences aside, because she wanted Duncan for herself. When he placed her on the bed, she held on to his shoulders. "Stay."

He kissed her and she caught his tongue, sucking it. She wanted to comfort him, to hold his head upon her breast and stroke him until the nervous energy within him eased. "Stay. Lie here beside me."

Duncan's expression was wary and uncertain. He closed his eyes and shook his head.

She'd actually told him to . . . to do several things. And he had, and now he wanted to carry all her wonderful moments out into the night. He wasn't going anywhere. Not if she could help it. Sybil locked her arms around his neck and tugged him over her. "There. Isn't that better?" she demanded as Duncan braced his arms tensely beside her head.

"For whom?" He shifted to one side and lay stiffly beside her.

Sybil yawned and laid her head on his shoulder. She nuzzled and pushed aside his shirt to find her skin, and pressed a kiss upon it. She burrowed her nose against the warm, smoothly covered muscle and decided to taste him. She licked him delicately. He tasted of soap and man with a bit of feverish salt tossed in. Quite delectable and her own homecoming present. "You taste good."

"Uh-huh."

Sybil skimmed out of her torn panty hose and cuddled closer to Duncan, who was lying straight and rigid. She pressed her breasts against his arm and looped her arms and legs around him. He was hers. "Stay put," she managed between yawns.

"Yes, ma'am."

Duncan's deep, husky tone curled around her like a warm, snugly blanket.

She dozed, and awoke with a silent scream on her lips. Sybil lay very still, willing away the nightmare. She could feel their rough hands on her...too many hands holding her down, parting her legs....

The sheets were tangled around her legs and the nightmare began to shred as she clung to reality. A night bird called and the summer wind brushed a limb against her window. The shadows of her bedroom gave way to the moonlight shafting into the room. There was the scent of the mountains, clean air and pine trees.

The ragged, deep groan beside her caused her heartbeat to kick up again. She turned to find Duncan sleeping beside her.

Sybil forced herself not to move. He sprawled on her cream-and-rosebud-spattered sheets, black hair gleaming on her pillow. A ruffle lay against his jaw—delicate lace against the hard line.

His thigh moved, hair coarse against her smooth skin.

Sybil eased the sheet up to her chin and pushed reality into her senses. Here she was, lying beside Duncan Tallchief without the benefit of a nightgown. She edged her leg away from his.

One glance downward proved that both of them were naked. A quick flood of memories swooped upon her and Sybil closed her eyes, shaking with the knowledge that Duncan had touched her as no other man had. She had even ordered him to...to taste her....

Duncan flung his forearm against his face. "Dad...Dad, I'm sorry...." The tortured cry had been wrenched from him; his tears shone in silvery trails down his cheek.

Comforting a grown man—a naked man—was far different from cuddling Emily.

His eyes flung open, staring sightlessly at her and filled with anguish. "Duncan?"

"Oh, God...I'm sorry...."

His tone was so shattered, so desperate, that Sybil reached to lay her hand on his cheek. He breathed quickly, still caught in his nightmare.

"Duncan?"

"I don't know if I can do it, Mom. But I'll try.... We'll stay together, the five of us. Mom?"

There were other frantic, jumbled sentences—a boy afraid of failing, fierce in his devotion to his family. She stroked his hair, hoping to relieve his nightmare. She saw then who Duncan was with his protection ripped away. He'd loved deeply, fought for those he loved.

"Duncan...come here...." Sybil eased his head to her breasts, rocking him, though his body almost covered hers. She welcomed the weight and kissed his forehead, holding him as gently as she would cradle Emily. "Duncan...shhh...."

Duncan sighed raggedly, tugging her close to him.

The next time Sybil surfaced from sleep, she heard the sound of her clothes dryer. She smelled brewing coffee and freshly showered male skin. She was being tucked in, kissed goodnight.

Still more asleep than awake, Sybil reached for him.

Duncan's deep voice whispered in her ear, "More?"

"Mmm, please." She stretched luxuriously and gave herself to the rhythmic movements within her. Pleasure came softly, pulsing, tightening within her, until she melted gloriously. "Thank you." She was, after all, very polite.

Duncan's rough cheek moved along her throat, his smile slow against her skin. There was nothing soft about his body curving behind hers.

"I don't know if I'm going to live through this."

She flopped over, afraid that he'd escape, and clung to him even as she drifted back into sleep. She'd trap him in flowers and ruffles and keep him safe from the shadows.

Seven

Duncan leaned against Sybil's kitchen counter, sipped his coffee and grimly tried to listen to Emily. The puppy chewed on his jeans; Duncan rolled him over gently, rubbing his sock-covered foot on the puppy's fat belly. Duncan would have rather been playing with a certain cuddly female.

Emily giggled and retrieved "Elvis." Duncan picked up bits about her calf, though his thoughts locked on the woman sleeping in a bed they had shared. Leaving Sybil just minutes earlier, removing himself from a luscious tangle of arms and legs, had been torture. His jeans were still damp from the dryer, and he wondered with humor if they steamed from the sensual heat gripping his entire body. Jerking on his socks, his shirt and a moderately welcoming expression for Emily hadn't been easy when every instinct and nerve he possessed told him to make love to Sybil.

In the morning light, Sybil's face had looked young and vulnerable, her lips slightly swollen. As she'd snuggled against him, her breasts had nudged his side, her soft leg sliding within his. She had very agile toes, walking them up and down his calf. She slept deeply, yet seemed in constant movement, arching and stretching luxuriously, which did little to calm Duncan's stretched nerves. But her cat-who-licked-the-cream smile and purrs did help.

Her delicate feminine petals had gently parted and moistly enfolded his touch. The need to sink deeply within her, to place himself within her tight, welcoming keeping, had risen too sharply. If he had moved with the heavy, primitive need surging through him, to thrust deep in her, spill himself into the tight pleasure, he might have hurt her, might have ruined what lay between them. He promised himself that the next time—

Emily spoke quietly while she sat on the floor, playing with her puppy and kitten. "Mom doesn't usually sleep this late. She must be really tired, because she works in the morning, when everything is quiet. I'm glad you came over this morning. You can see what she brought me. But I'm just glad she's home."

Calum, who had brought Emily over from Elspeth's, sprawled in a chair. He met Duncan's eyes; the understanding look held between the two brothers. "You know what you're doing, then," Calum said finally, and Duncan nodded.

A sleepy, deeply pleased feminine sigh slid from Sybil's bedroom into the morning. Calum's expression was humorous as he eyed Duncan and whispered, "The least you can do for the woman is button your shirt straight and put on your boots."

Emily, a younger version of Sybil, glanced at Duncan and studied his morning beard. She watched him slowly correct his buttons and holes and then looked at him. The girl was soft and sweet, yet the intuitive woman moved within her, shadowing her expression with understanding beyond her years. Duncan met her gaze with his steady one. There was nothing light in his feelings for her mother; his attraction was not a passing whim. The girl understood as she watched him and stroked her kitten. "I like to wear socks when I'm at home," she said finally in a quiet way he recognized.

Though Sybil might not want his presence this morning—or would she?—her daughter accepted and trusted him. Emily had picked her way through her reservations.

The bedroom door opened, and Sybil, her glasses askew and hair rippling wildly, stood in her new robe.

While Sybil stretched and yawned, Duncan shot a look at Calum. His brother was innocently studying the plaster design on the ceiling.

She blinked when she saw Duncan and jabbed her finger up to straighten her glasses, then she shook her head as if to clear it.

Duncan wasn't budging. If she wanted him to give her reassurance that last night hadn't happened, that she hadn't melted beneath his touch, hadn't pulled him into her bed, she was out of luck. And if she thought he'd run before dawn, she could think again.

Calum whistled a soft tune as Sybil tried to awake fully.

"Mom?" Emily jumped to her feet and ran to Sybil, enfolding her in hugs and kisses. Then Emily was bounding out the door to the car, anxious for her gift.

Sybil looked blankly at Duncan, then at Calum and back at Duncan. Her eyes widened and he watched a delicious shade of pink move up her throat. She scrunched the lapels of her robe over her breasts and swished the material to conceal her legs.

Duncan wondered if she regretted letting him touch her. If she regretted the closeness during the night. He inhaled and fought to remember what secret he had released, a memory that taunted him and danced beyond his recognition. He remembered his desperation, the pain, then the softness of Sybil holding him, whispering to him, easing him.

"I have to go—a trip to San Francisco. A hacker has infiltrated a security system and planted a worm—a computer bug—in it. It's eating its way through the company's memory banks. There's a hefty bonus tagged on to the offer, if I can nail the virus quickly." Calum rose, downed the last of his coffee and kissed Sybil on her forehead. Outside he spoke quietly to Emily.

Duncan handed Sybil a cup of coffee, then smoothed back a tousled length of warm, silky hair. She stepped back against the wall warily, looking up at him through glasses now steamed with coffee. He didn't trust what he saw in her eyes and placed a hand beside her head, blocking her slide away from him. "Good morning."

"Uh...good morning." She watched Emily and Calum through the window. "Ah...my, isn't it a pretty morning?" Sybil swallowed tightly and edged her coffee cup between them. Her fingers trembled on the cup.

"Sleep well?" Duncan wound a curl around his finger and tugged. He wanted her now, there on the sun-warmed tile of the kitchen floor. He allowed no room between them, taking her cup and placing it aside.

Her voice was very tight; the pulse in her throat pounded wildly against his fingertip. Her flush ran deeper.

"Quite well, thank you."

"You smile—a small, secretive and very-pleased-with-yourself smile—when you sleep. It's a sight a man appreciates and one to drive him mad. Those little purrs don't help, either."

"I must have been dreaming— You watched me?" Her bottom lip dropped open and she stared blankly up at him.

Duncan wasn't in the mood for giving her room to escape. He trailed his finger across her cheek and found the sharp row of her teeth. A tap on her chin and he followed the path of his finger down her throat, tracing the robe to the crevice between her breasts. "I watched you. Watched everything. I'm not likely to forget the heat inside you, not when I'm dying to have you. I want to bury myself so deep in you that we're one body and you're hot and tight around me. For a man, it's a beautiful thing to see a woman's body capture and hold tightly on to pleasure he's given her."

"I'm not certain that was gallant of you, Duncan. To watch me...you know."

Her unsteady, husky reply seemed so proper; a fragile, cool lily beside the raw tension humming within him. "Come to the house. I'd like you to see the cradle. I've cleaned away the old layers of varnish." Duncan could feel her sliding away from him, setting her barriers in place.

What had happened last night? What had slipped from his keeping into hers? Or had it?

"Old things, brought to life by those who care, are beautiful." Her whisper trembled on the cool, morning air. She lifted her finger to stroke his cheekbone, to feather across his lashes—

The screen door crashed open and Emily yelled, "Mom. Guess who's here? Gavin! Isn't that great?"

Duncan sheltered Sybil a moment, sensed her grasping at her proper moorings, and then he turned. The man dressed in an expensive suit and tie matched Duncan for height, but not for raw muscle. His stylish glasses glinted as he took in Duncan from head to toe—unshaven and standing in his socks near Sybil, who looked thoroughly mussed.

The man, younger than Duncan, bore just the cool class that would suit Sybil, while Duncan's raw edges could scrape her polish. He didn't like the man's quick frown, or the tensing of his body. Duncan recognized the protective stance in the man and the menace springing behind the mirror-like glasses. Duncan stood very still, keeping Sybil partly behind him.

Sybil's elbow nudged Duncan sharply as she stepped around him. He put out a hand and caught the sash at the back of her robe; he wasn't ready to share her yet. Especially with a man more suited to Sybil than himself.

The hair on Duncan's nape lifted as he recognized that this man fitted somehow into Sybil's life.

The man took a step forward, and Duncan tensed at his words.

"Sybil? Are you all right?"

He cared deeply; his fists closed at his thighs, his expression threatening Duncan. Duncan moved forward to the challenge, his chest meeting Sybil's back.

She shook free and stood very straight in front of him. He sensed that she was protecting the other man. Duncan rummaged through his battered emotions and found that he'd enjoy tearing the city from the man. He took a step forward and Sybil braced back against him, staying his movement.

"Gavin! How nice to see you."

"Sybil." Gavin's tight tone lacked warmth, his blue eyes locked with Duncan's. The city boy wasn't flabby. Nor was he backing up.

Sybil looked up at Duncan, then over to Gavin. "I, ah . . ."

Her hands pushed frantically at her mussed hair flying everywhere. Duncan blew a silky strand from his nose as she spoke.

"Ah...Gavin, this is Duncan Tallchief. You remember how I told you he had rescued Emily. He's...ah...just here to..."

She glanced down at Duncan's sock-covered feet, glued to her kitchen tile, and she floundered, clearly ashamed of what had passed. "Umm. Duncan, this is Gavin James. He's... an old friend... we were once engaged. Would you mind pouring him coffee while I dress?"

Thorn pushed through the screen door, carrying his bowl. Duncan had forgotten the dog during the night and Thorn had apparently made the trip back to the ranch to retrieve his favorite food dish. He plopped it at Sybil's feet, looking up at her expectantly. His nose lifted at an unfamiliar human scent. Then, stiff-legged, his hackles raised, he bared his fangs at Gavin and growled.

Duncan saw Sybil's topaz eyes flash meaningfully up at him and then down at his dog. Beast and master had reacted instinctively to the new man in Sybil's house.

She scratched the animal's ears, then straightened. "Shame on you. This is Gavin. Duncan, has Thorn been outside all night? Ah..." Sybil placed a trembling hand over her mouth. She evaluated her escape routes—shielding Duncan's presence in her house—and came up with "Mmm. Duncan, would you please...?"

Duncan looked at her. On the morning after sharing Sybil's bed, he didn't feel like being civilized. He glanced at Thorn, who was still baring his teeth at Gavin. He knew exactly how his dog felt. Damned if he'd serve coffee and a smile to an ex-fiancé. Especially to a lover who probably had seen several delicious smiles. Who may have created them. Duncan fought the need to pit himself against something, and Gavin James was the closest— "No."

Then he scooped up his boots and walked out of her house.

"I have my vices," Elspeth admitted as the two women sat on the floor of her living room. "Saturday night. Old movies and a tub of buttered popcorn from the theater. How much better can it get?"

After two weeks of seeing Duncan at almost every turn, Sybil wasn't in a good mood. An encounter with the hard wall of his chest at the post office had almost caused her to latch both arms onto his neck and kiss that grim, accusing line of his mouth. He'd behaved as if she were having a convention of lovers in her kitchen. "You should have seen Duncan that morning. Gavin was no better. At any minute I thought my kitchen would be splattered in blood.... There was no reason for Duncan to act like a territorial male. None at all. Your brother is a rat. No offense, Elspeth."

"None taken. Duncan has been bristling nicely. You're doing a good job of payback. The women who have hunted him are rooting for you."

Sybil, comfortable in black shorts and matching T-shirt, studied Elspeth, who was also dressed in black. Both women had black streaks beneath their eyes—a camouflage trick, according to Elspeth. Sybil fingered her single, long braid, which matched Elspeth's. "Who would believe that you would lead me into crime?"

"Lori's ex-husband is being a rat. He's always been one and I didn't like him waving that ... woman in front of his kids. Especially when they're on visitation with him and he's paying absolutely no attention to them. He's just hurting Lori for meanness, not because he wants the children. It seemed only fair to lure that skunk in his sports car, one Lori helped pay for." Elspeth swigged her bottle of flavored mineral water and burped delicately.

This facet of Elspeth—walking on the wild side—fascinated Sybil. "You are wicked. I can't believe I helped you. He'll find the popcorn trail to the car."

"No way. The skunk ate it." Elspeth shook loose her gleaming hair from the braid. It spilled down her back, catching the light in blue-black sparks. "You've got to do something about those two anonymous telephone calls."

"I'll deal with them. They aren't very creative, a limited sexually explicit verbiage of what he'd do to me. I had the unpleasant experience before ... years ago." *Just after the rape. The voices were muffled, threatening her....* She forced herself back to the present. "I can't believe I actually held that gunnysack while you looted Mr. Lockison's beautiful garden."

Another delicate burp and a fond grin. "The things I learned from Fiona. Mr. Lockison pulled so many shady deals with his renters that they deserved a portion of his garden."

"I can't believe we spied on John Wade. Last night, we actually took out our field glasses, lay in the grass and watched him—uh—sneak into Mrs. Snodgrass's house."

In the light of the television screen, Elspeth's expression lacked pity. "He's there every Saturday night, just when he tells his wife he's out checking on his livestock. Mr. Snodgrass, as a deputy, is usually patrolling the other side of town at that time. Wade has blackmailed and harassed his last defenseless and down-on-her-luck woman. I'm merely documenting his visits around town. All it will take is a careful notation to each of his girlfriends and the cat is out of the bag. Oh, no names of course, except Wade's. That way poor, sweet Mrs. Wade just may be kept in the dark."

Sybil lifted her bottle of mineral water in a toast. "A supreme plan. Congratulations."

"Thank you. As I said, everything I know, I learned from my brothers and Fiona, who is marvelous on a caper. A real intuitive player. She'll be in Arizona for a bit longer, apparently locked on to the mother lode of causes." Elspeth tilted her head, listening. "That is Duncan's pickup. He must be just back from the cattlemen's meeting. He's taken a special interest in benefits for a disabled girl and her parents."

"Forget I'm here, will you?" Sybil hugged a sofa pillow to her and tried not to ache for the sight of Duncan Tallchief.

His boots sounded on the back porch and Elspeth welcomed him. In the next instant the lights clicked on in the living room and Duncan stood with his arms across his chest. "Hello, Duncan," she managed. Just. How like him to leave his hat on, looking more like a desperado than when she'd met him.

A civilized man would have called her to discuss the scene in her kitchen. They could have had dinner and talked. Duncan preferred to glare at her as if she'd committed a crime. After holding her, touching her so beautifully, he could have shown some sensitivity to her first-time awakening to him—and a houseful of people, including her daughter and an old friend. Sybil chose to ignore him now—a difficult task, considering how glad she'd been to see him that night. Just how many times did he think she had reacted to a man like that, opening herself to him? She shot a dark look at him and found him returning it. How could she ever expect him to act like a gentleman?

"Fine. The two of you, dressed in burglar black and crowing over your capers with popcorn and old movies. Where's Emily?" The edge in his tone wasn't exactly cuddling.

"At a slumber party. Go away." She hugged the pillow tighter. She resented Duncan breaching the mother-daughter duet and playing the role of a father. Emily was her daughter alone and Duncan's tone implied he had rights. He didn't. With her or with Emily.

"I've come to let Elspeth cut my hair," he returned smugly, daring her to challenge his right to be there. He tipped back his hat and hooked his thumbs in his belt. "Unless you want to."

Sybil rose carefully to her feet and never looked away from him. There he stood, all six foot four of male arrogance, offering to let her cut his hair. To serve him. "I could do a very good job. Right down to your hard skin."

"Skin is good."

Duncan's reply was too slow and taunting, and every inch of her heated, as she remembered his hands running over her body.

"How's dear Gavin-boy?" he asked in a ruthless drawl.

He hadn't forgotten. With his glinting, narrowed eyes and widespread legs, locked at the knee, Duncan that morning would have put western gunfighters to shame. Now he was facing her in that same *High Noon* stance, waiting for her to make the first move. She threw up her hands. "If there is one man who can spoil a beautiful evening, it's you. I feel absolutely no reason to explain anything to you. You could have stayed and been nice."

"Nice." The word cut the air between them. "Yes. I could have stayed and shown off my manners. We could all have been very civil."

He smiled slowly, a wolfish, all-too-knowing smirk that brought the hair on the nape of her neck standing straight up. How like him to seek her out when she wasn't expecting him and when her defenses were down. Duncan jerked down the brim of his hat, shadows shielding his face.

One more second and she'd show him— Summoning every shred of the ladylike behavior she possessed, Sybil stood very straight. "Elspeth, thank you for the lovely evening. I'm going home."

He caught her arm as she swished by him. The pad of his thumb swooped and came away with the black beneath her eyes. His expression softened. "You look like Fiona, all filled with herself after a raid and ready to take down the first one who stands in her way. Who would believe that sweet Elspeth and her cool accomplice would make friends with skunks and raid gardens?"

"Next time you can help, Duncan. Now, come sit down and behave," Elspeth ordered, as if he were a little boy.

There was nothing innocent about the way Duncan's eyes raked Sybil's T-shirt. "Miss me?" he asked too softly, then scooped her against him and bent to take a swift, hungry kiss.

Sybil managed to walk home, her legs unsteady. Duncan's kiss had not been sweet or tender. It was a claiming and a challenge; she could either run or she could fight.

Marcella Portway's ancestry lacked any relationship to Spain. In the next week, Sybil had launched an all-out campaign to catch up on work and find the link to Marcella's desired royal ancestry. Indications so far were that Marcella would have to cancel plans to visit her homeland and castle.

Duncan's brooding cowboy image seemed pasted on Sybil's computer screen and the devastating kiss couldn't be unpeeled from her lips. Nor could his challenge.

After a blistering forty-five minutes, Sybil had been too curt with a well-known client. Pleased clients had led to better business; disgruntled ones could ruin her as easily. Marcella also tossed in the fact that there would be a handsome incentive if Sybil verified the link. She had added that Sybil's parents, in her elite social circle, would be also pleased. That sly reference to the strained relationship between Sybil and her family was little more than blackmail.

If Mr. Wade could be defeated, so could Marcella. "You'll have to find someone else, Mrs. Portway. I'll be happy to send you the files with my contacts so far. You might be interested to know that I did find an ancestor of yours who was a murderer. Then there's the French horse thief and rapist and the English one who was branded a coward. One of your grandmothers worked in a—she was a working woman who specialized in sailors.''

Marcella gasped, muttered a threat, and Sybil glanced outside. With Elspeth at a trade show, she was left with Elspeth's blackmailing project. Already dressed in black, she wove her hair into a single braid. With Emily spending another night at a slumber party, it would soon be her turn to host the giggling girls. It would be her first time as a hosting mother. "Good evening, Mrs. Portway. Better luck elsewhere.''

Forty-five minutes later, Sybil lay on the grass, her binoculars in place along with her notepad. Her mini-flashlight's beam caught Elspeth's neat handwriting: "For All Women Everywhere.'' Apparently defending the helpless ran in the Tallchiefs' gene pool. What else could be expected of the descendants of a noble chieftain and a wild-tempered Scotswoman?

She watched a familiar car circle the block and slide into the shadows to park discreetly. The lights in Mrs. Snodgrass's bedroom window blinked off; the stage was set. For a small town, Amen Flats was certainly busy.

The wind rustled the grass nearby as Sybil scanned the quiet town. Birk's pickup was parked at Maddy's and Lacey's motorcycle stood against the curb.

A firm nudge at her hips caused her to flip to her back. Duncan stood over her. "I might have known. Elspeth is out of town. Having fun?''

From her angle, lying flat on the ground, he looked a mile high, his hat shading his face. There was nothing easy in the wide stance of his long legs or his boots locked in the grass.

With the exception of her two escapades with Elspeth, Sybil had absolutely never done anything shady. "Ah...I was just...ah...'' She glanced around and found huge shapes looming in the moonlight. She hadn't known they were there, but since they were she might as well use them. "I was just studying the nocturnal habits of the buffalo. You know there are two kinds, the plains and the smaller black buffalo. Of course, the plains are larger, and—according to theory—then when the herd was almost extinct they cross-bred. Tracing the gene pools back to the original species is quite difficult—"

Duncan bent, latched a big fist to her black sweater and hefted her to her feet. He handled her weight easily, as though she were a child. No one had manhandled Sybil—with the exception of— She tried to dislodge his fist; it didn't move. Duncan did things on his terms and slowly released her. A woman who controlled her life and set her own terms, Sybil managed to hold her temper to a rumbling-volcano level. "I really don't like being manhandled, Duncan."

He grimly watched her dust herself free of leaves and grass. "Suit yourself. But one wrong move or a sound and that herd would make mincemeat out of you."

She wished she hadn't taken an instinctive step closer to him. "Uh...I thought Elspeth said they were more pets than wild."

Duncan picked a leaf from her breast and dropped it between them. "Right. Elspeth also knows a thing called keeping downwind and how to move and talk with them around. Is this where she said to be?"

"No...I could see better here...uh...Duncan?" Sybil peered around his shoulder to the huge shadow lumbering toward them.

His curse was short and disgusted. In the next minute, he'd scooped Sybil up in his arms and was running across the field. The heartbeat after he stopped, Duncan jerked her up against him and took her mouth.

Duncan threw his hat to a table and ripped off his gloves. Less than an hour ago, he'd manhandled Sybil. One look at the buffalo bull catching her scent and seeing the rest of the herd follow Old Apache toward her was enough to freeze Duncan's blood. He'd acted instinctively and reaction to his fear— that she could have been harmed—had caused the kiss.

So much for a man who knew how to cuddle frightened, crying, lost children and make them feel safe.

Handling a woman like Sybil should be like touching fragile silk. He looked down at his big, scarred, work-roughened hands. "Way to go, Tallchief."

Every nurturing instinct he possessed told him that within Sybil lurked a girl just budding into sexual awareness. She'd been scarred badly at a critical time and tossed away by parents with hearts of ice. Elspeth and Fiona probably had better growing-up times, though they resented their protective older brothers.

Just looking at Sybil caused Duncan to go hard.

He ran the back of his hand across his upper lip and found sweat. A celibate man, he'd missed thousands of national averages in the sexual department and not another woman had stirred him.

Duncan unbuttoned his shirt, dragged air into his lungs and leaned against the wall. Until the old bull moved, Duncan had been admiring the neat curve of Sybil's backside. He'd been remembering the few hours spent with her snuggling that bare softness against him.

Beside the fireplace, the old cradle gleamed softly in the moonlight. *The woman who brings the cradle to a man of Fearghus blood will fill it with his babies....*

Duncan snorted in disbelief, pushing himself away from the wall. He moved to the fireplace and placed a boot on the hearth. The old barn board with the Tallchief brand stood on the mantel and Duncan traced the burned outline. The stick man had lines radiating from the head, signifying a full headdress. The brand lying beside the board was a remnant of cattle drives. There was a bit of red where Fiona had dipped the brand into paint and marked her calf. He gripped the hearth and remembered how he had planned to ask Sybil to go out with him. For her, he'd drag out his rusty manners and try his best at acting civilized.

He had no right to want Sybil.

They weren't a good match. He'd seen that clearly when Gavin James had arrived.

There was no way he could rein in his desire to possess and to protect her.

He had to protect her from himself, because around her his control slid to his boots.

Duncan ran his hand through his hair. She'd been handled roughly and was incredibly fragile, yet he was acting like the animals who had wounded her.

Her smile as she'd slept haunted him day and night. Duncan kicked the stone hearth lightly. A woman like Sybil had no idea of the raw passions stirring him.

Or that he felt like a half-grown boy, high on love, just looking at her.

A man used to western sounds and the silence of Tallchief Mountain, Duncan caught the sound of a motor revving in the distance. He turned to look out upon the fields below the house and saw headlights shooting into the night. Whoever had come to see him drove like a bat out of—

Duncan inhaled unsteadily. Sybil had picked a bad night to haul her classy but cute rear to his ranch. He watched, amused, as her car stopped, the headlights outlining cattle. They milled around the car as she honked, and Duncan shook his head. A city woman in the middle of the Tallchief spread was asking for trouble. In another minute the old longhorn bull would charge the noise—

Duncan almost started out the door to the pasture. His horse would save time, if Sybil didn't start a stampede first. Duncan stopped, his hand locked to his hat. Her headlights still on, Sybil eased around the old longhorn bull and began walking toward the ranch house. One thrust of those long, sharply curved horns and Sybil— A huge, icy fist slammed into his gut.

Duncan moved quickly to his front porch and saw Sybil move safely away from the herd. He silenced his dog with a low whistle. Thorn, more wolf than dog, whined. His tail thumped the floor and his yellow eyes looked up to Duncan, waiting for the command *go*. "Lay off—she's not coming to pay a social call," Duncan ordered as Sybil marched up the road.

She searched him out in the shadows as though she knew where he'd be found. She scowled at him as she continued, hair floating from her face, framing the sweep of her cheekbones, the lift of her chin.

He knew he'd never see the sight again…a red-haired witch come calling on him, flouncing up his road wearing nothing but her temper and the Tallchief plaid. It ran across her breasts and over one very stiff, pale shoulder.

"Don't say one word. Not one." She didn't pause at his front steps, but continued walking past him. Was that steam coming from her body? Or a moonbeam waiting to slide down it? He envied the moonlight crossing into the room to touch her. He followed her into the living room, where she stood before the hearth in the Tallchief tartan plaid and western boots.

"That's quite a picture." Duncan breathed unsteadily and knew he'd remember the sight forever.

She threw up a hand, signaling him to stop talking. The other hand latched on to the old cradle.

He saw the other half of himself there, the woman fierce in her anger and tethered to the cradle. *The woman who brings the cradle to a man of Fearghus blood will fill it with his babies....* Duncan's heart lurched into rapid pace.

"You have no idea at all how to treat a lady."

"Have you come courting me, sweetheart?" he heard himself drawl, though every nerve within his body stretched painfully. "Because if not, you're in the wrong place at the wrong time. Sweet Jesus. Aren't you wearing anything under that getup?" he demanded rawly.

"Not a stitch. I've come to meet your challenge, Mr. Duncan Tallchief. So far, you've had things all your way. Now I want equal terms." She pointed a finger at him. "Your trouble is you have an empty nest syndrome. You've raised your brood and now you're searching for someone to tuck under your wing. I've been taking care of myself for years. Count me out."

"The hell I will." He wanted to fill his bed with the woman standing in front of him. Instinct told him that she wasn't finished, and if ever he should rein himself in, it had to be now. Sybil was calling him out.

He moved to the hearth to get a better view of anything curved and feminine beneath the tartan. He caught a rounded hip and a triangular shadow above one thigh— Duncan locked his shaking hands to his belt. He was afraid he'd say the wrong thing, touch her too hungrily....

"This could get rough. You had better tell Thorn to wait outside. I don't want his feelings hurt. And don't count on him for protection from me." Sybil stayed put until Duncan had complied and returned to the fireplace.

She'd come for him. He balanced his hunger and his fears and decided that he'd better clamp down any impulse to touch her. He wanted her desperately enough to let her make her choices. This time. For a man like Duncan, the decision wasn't easy.

Sybil tossed her hair back. "I'm very angry with you, Tallchief. You absolutely lack everything that is redeeming in the other members of your family. Oh, I haven't met Fiona, of course, but I like the sound of her. Because your sisters won't allow you to bully them, don't think you can pick on me. If I want to lie on the grass at night, I will. I might just pet a buffalo."

Two thousand pounds or more of buffalo and she wanted to pet one? He decided not to pose the challenge to her. In her present mood, she might walk her western boots and the Tallchief tartan right up to Old Apache. He tried a safer route. "Your binoculars were glinting in the moonlight, sweetheart. I saw you from the road. If Wade had his mind with him, he could have seen you easily."

"Details."

Sybil began to pace in front of him and every molecule in Duncan's body told him to carry her to his bed. She continued stalking in front of him, allowing him a glance at a sleek thigh, quickly shielded.

"Emily is deeply attached to you. If you planned to use her to get to me...no, discount that. Your style is a direct hit. You swoop, Duncan Tallchief. SWOOP, in big capital letters. Oh, yes. Skip the wine and dine and dancing bit, the companionship, the relationship, and get straight to those devastating kisses."

She stopped pacing and faced him. "Oh, yes. As if you didn't know it. Your kisses aren't wet or sloppy. They're just there—swoop, bang, whop, mesmerizing. It's unfair. Okay...okay. The point is that you've been treating me like a minor partner. I'm not one of your siblings, one of your brood to care for, Duncan. I am a woman who has had to rely on herself. I've survived. Giving you a small portion of control over me isn't easy. Small? You want everything and it's too much without a balance in return. I refuse unequal terms in our relationship. Now, get this—"

Sybil slid the tartan from her body and folded it slowly while he watched, mouth drying and heart locked between beats. Delicately formed, Sybil's body curved perfectly, her breasts tilted to peaks in the moonlight, her waist small enough for his two hands. There was a rounded hip and a softly molded belly and then the dark mystery above her thighs. Enchanting him, she moved in a symphony of shyness, determination and defiance. The combination started his blood heating, pouring through him, and he wondered if his jeans could bear the strain.

At the last, she held the folded cloth against her, protectively, her breasts raised by the pressure.

Duncan knew a heavy pressure of his own as she sent him a curious look, her lashes fluttering down upon her hot cheeks. She'd taken her time and was tucking away the last of her doubts with the cloth. He owed her that—the gentle time of a woman—choosing her path. His own had been forged from the moment they'd met, when she'd come flying across Maddy's to claim him. Duncan held himself still, fighting his steely need for her.

He wondered whether his heart would leap into her keeping if she reached out a hand to him.

She smoothed the cloth into the cradle and stood slowly in front of him. She raised her chin, a fighter like him, setting her terms and fighting her fears. Duncan fought the need to hold her, to reassure her. But it was no easy matter for the both of them, and his hunting instincts told him to wait.

He traced the luminous pools of her eyes and found what he wanted: the steel to match his own. She held herself with pride, a woman who knew her mind.

Sybil's hair glowed around her, all silk and silver and scented waves spilling like a waterfall around her shoulders. "So here I am. I've determined that you may be the type of male who has to be dealt with on a base level, then work up from that. You've evidently inherited some of your grandfather's tendencies to pluck women up and run with them, discounting that the woman in question may have ideas of her own.... I've never done this before and it's crazy." She rubbed her forehead as if to clear it. "I don't have the slightest idea how to proceed—"

He caught her to him, leaving her no room to fly. "Is this what you want?"

"Desperately, Duncan." Then she began to grin. A giggle followed. "You look so...desperate and dangerous. I...I'm nervous...I detest being tossed over your shoulder and I wish I could do the same right now and why don't you kiss me and why don't we...ah...well...I've decided to take the bull by the horns or...ah...uh...you know. I thought if making love is such a problem that we could get that out of the way first and work from there. I mean the other night, I...you...it wasn't fair. I have never come after a man in my life, never wanted one badly enough."

"Let me get this straight. Are you offering yourself to me?" He realized he sounded too rough, too demanding.

She smiled shyly, and the tight knot inside Duncan began unfurling. "I'm nervous. I'm afraid I'll ruin this by being afraid." She looked away and he prayed she wasn't changing her mind. "Gavin understood...."

"I'm not him. Lay it out."

She ran her fingers through her wild hair, tears shimmering in her eyes before she dashed them away. He waited for her to run, waited for the pain—

Instead, Sybil stood on tiptoe to kiss him lightly.

"I won't hurt you," he heard himself whisper unsteadily, easing his arms around her so as not to frighten her.

"I know.... Oh, Duncan. You're shaking...."

Eight

Duncan promised himself he'd be very gentle, very slow with Sybil.

Then her hand floated downward, just skimming the hair veeing down his stomach. He sucked in his breath as her fingers toyed with his buckle. Both of Sybil's hands tried and failed to open his belt. Duncan groaned, unable to look away from her fingers fluttering upon him. He ripped open his belt buckle in one flip and met Sybil's nibbling kisses. They were sweet and cool and untutored and her fingers traced his jeans snap— Duncan tugged away the snap, leaving her to find his zipper.

She slowly slid the zipper downward....

"Leave the driving to me." Sybil's husky, uneven whisper almost caused Duncan to laugh. She kissed the curve of his lips and hesitantly touched the very tip of him.

He knew she needed to explore his body. She'd been forced, raped. Then from her actions, Duncan knew that her marriage had not been a tender one. On a sensual level, Sybil was young, and untried, and needed time to understand that his hunger, his body, was only that of a man who valued her. If she needed to explore him to satisfy her curiosity, and to reckon with her needs, he'd—

"Would you mind if we rested a bit?" he managed, just as she found the shape of him, pressing gently.

"Why?"

He sucked in more air and held his body taut. One more touch and— "I'm having a little difficulty with your project."

Her eyes raised to his, all innocence with her busy fingers purely sinful upon him. "Project?"

"You're getting to me, Sybil," he admitted grimly. He pulled back slightly, holding her away from him. In the moonlight, her breasts were tilted sweetly upward. He bent to gently nip and kiss each one. They were like shy, sweet doves, coming to shelter within the safety of his hands. "One more minute of those curious fingers and I can't promise anything."

Sybil trembled, her head back, her eyes almost closed. "Good."

He found his desire reflected in her expression, in the slow sweep of her tongue across her lips, moistening them. He ran his thumb across the taut bud of her breast, watched her inhale, then slowly, carefully, rolled her nipple between his finger and thumb. She shivered, her fingers digging into his upper arms. He breathed in her scent and admitted rawly, "I don't think I can make it to the bedroom."

"Good."

He counted her "goods," hoarded them. Still holding his gaze, Sybil began to ease to the floor and he followed her. He prayed his body wouldn't betray him, that he wouldn't—

He groaned as she parted her thighs, cradling him close to her. Her heat fairly burned him, beckoning.... Duncan stroked her hair away from her face, letting her set the pace. Slowly....

Bracing his weight from her, just enough to let her breasts drag softly upon his chest, to nestle against him, he pressed his hips down gently. She'd been taken too roughly once and he wanted her to know that he wouldn't hurt her. Duncan framed her face with his hands. "We've got all the time you need, sweetheart. I'll be very careful with you. Tell me what you want and we can stop when you want. You're so small there, so tight."

Sybil found him and with one arch of her hips took him deeply within her. She cried out, and shocked, Duncan slid deeper until he thought he'd touch the very heart of her. "Are you hurt?"

Damn. He'd promised her. He was too rough with her.

Then he watched her smile slowly, her lashes sweeping along her flushed cheeks. Her hands caressed his taut back, his buttocks and down his thighs. Duncan had heard of women claiming men, and with her arms and legs binding him, her body tight and moist and hot around him, he knew that he'd been claimed to the hilt.

He watched her intently, her expressions reflected in her luminous eyes. He read tenderness and discovery, like a rosebud opening to a new day. He pushed back her hair, stroked her temples with his thumbs and kept her safe as she chose each heartbeat to stay with him. To let her know that he understood, that there was more than the meeting of their bodies, Duncan drifted kisses upon her lashes, her forehead, nose and cheek. "Stay with me," he whispered close to her ear, his heart fusing with the wild fluttering of hers. "You're so tight, so hot.... Let me in. I won't hurt you."

The smile playing around her lips told him her secret: that she had captured him and had her way. While her body eased to accept his, Sybil breathed deeply, her fingernails pressing into his shoulders. She flexed delicately, flowing beneath him, and Duncan knew he'd never made love like this, a tender game. She smoothed his taut shoulders as he tried to draw back and found himself taken too tightly to move. She seemed very pleased with herself, and if he wasn't mistaken—his world had just soared off into the moon—her feminine muscles were gently squeezing and releasing him. "You pounced."

"Yep. Swoop and took. You're not going anywhere." Though her tone said she was pleased with herself, Sybil frowned slightly.

He found himself grinning as she squirmed and adjusted to him; he treasured her determination. As the object of her concentration, he felt obliged to offer, "If you're uncomfortable, I can leave."

"I'm in control here, Tallchief. What's the process—Ohh...." Sybil arched her hips higher and cried out softly. She trembled, slowly lowering her body from his, only to rise sharply again. He treasured the tiny constrictions tugging at him and prayed his body would obey his will. Sybil's hands ran softly over him like the brush of rose petals. "I thought this would be horribly painful. It isn't. I ... must have been thinking that it would be the same."

He mourned for the girl and cherished the woman. "You were ready for me. There's a difference. For my part, there is minor pain."

"Oh, Duncan! I didn't mean to hurt you ... it just felt so right—so good." She raised her hips again and he groaned again. Pleasure had tossed her against him, her face taut with it. "Duncan? Duncan?"

He tried to wait, but the moist tightening within her set him off. He tried to tell her something, his words thundering—or was it his blood? This was Sybil—scents; feminine muscles; sweet, hungry kisses ... this was his woman ... a part of him as no other woman had been....

The shadows were gone and he was warm....

He found her breast, suckling, nipping, catching her bottom in his hands and lifting her, pouring into her. What he was, he wanted to be with her ... to join with her. He fought his release and failed, heard Sybil cry out, her mouth against his throat. What was she saying? What was she saying?

She flung out her hand to grip the cradle, to tether them to it, and Duncan placed his hand over hers, a pledge to keep her safe.

The pounding of his blood echoed throughout the flashing colors of fire, higher....

"I love you. Oh, Duncan ... I love you so much...."

Had her lips formed the words? Or did he want them so much he imagined them? Did her heart race to meet his?

After the pounding heat he held very still, listening, sensing, feeling as though he had completed a full circle. She was what had been missing in his heart, and she was his alone and he was hers. Sybil brushed back his hair from his forehead ...

Warm. Sweet. Soft. Unwilling to release the missing part of himself, this tender captive, Duncan settled upon her, bracing his full weight from her. Their hands remained locked on the cradle; neither one had the strength to release it. With his thumb, he stroked the smooth skin on the back of her hand.

"You looked so fierce, so powerful," she whispered against his damp forehead.

"Was." He tried to breathe. He kissed her shoulder and smelled deeply of her fragrance.

"You're a pussycat, Mr. Tallchief."

"Thanks, I do my best. I've been saving up for this." If he had had to move one toe, he couldn't have found the strength.

"It was right." She turned her hand to his, intertwining her fingers with his as he brought her hand to his lips and kissed the back.

He must have dozed, his head upon her breasts. Her heart slowed from its furious pace and he luxuriously stroked the curve of her hip. Half-asleep and very relaxed, Duncan decided there were advantages to letting a woman make up her mind. He weighed the pluses of being Sybil's captive, her raid successful. He was just summoning energy for a raid of his own, when she whispered against his ear, "You know, I could be highly fertile—"

Duncan's long lashes lifted instantly; they swept along her skin and tickled. His formerly hard body, draped so pleasantly over her, tensed. She could almost hear him thinking, damning himself for not using protection. But she didn't want him to say anything to ruin her moment. Their moment. When everything had healed within her.

Duncan moved suddenly, drawing her with him to stand. He lifted her into his arms and carried her up the stairway, taking them two at a time. In seconds, they were standing beneath the shower and he was soaping her very gently. His hand moved between her thighs. She should have been embarrassed; she wasn't. She felt lighthearted and young and thoroughly enjoyed Duncan's absolute mortification.

"I should know better," he said.

"I think it's my time to conceive." She slid the second volley of her idea to him on a platter of steam and spraying water. Gripping the cradle with his hand over hers while they had made love had caused brilliant images. Once she'd gotten past the shooting stars. Duncan, for all his raw edges, would be a perfect father.

Duncan closed his eyes, water glistening on his jutting cheekbones and dripping from his forehead to his lashes. When he opened his lids, his expression was tender. "I'm not certain, but you're teasing me, right? This is some odd humor from a redheaded witch who came strolling into my house to— Making a baby is a serious business, woman. If things are right between a man and a woman, and they want children, it's the most important thing a man can do in his lifetime."

There it was, the warrior laying down the law, addressing her as "woman."

Sybil shrugged inwardly. She certainly felt like Duncan Tallchief's woman. Very well-loved and treasured.

"For a big man, you move quite quickly when frightened." She couldn't help laughing at his dazed expression. Unprotected sex shouldn't happen, but she was glad. In fact, she was flying. All the parts of her that hadn't made sense with Duncan leaped into a straight, logical line. She'd wanted him from the first moment she'd seen him brawling. He was hers to claim and she had. Faint heart did not apply to her actions tonight. "The next time, I'll give notice before I pounce."

"Do that." He continued to lave soap down her body, treating her breasts ever so gently. He kissed a red mark, his expression dark with regret. "I promised I wouldn't hurt you."

"You didn't." Sybil stood very still, entranced by this tall, tender man who had tended others before himself. She felt she was being worshipped, that he had placed aside everything but her. Beneath his care, she believed that only she was truly a unique woman to him. She pressed his hands against her breasts, kept them there and lifted her lips. Duncan's kiss exceeded her expectations, soft, seeking . . .

He hadn't given himself lightly, nor had she, and tonight would be the start of—

Sybil jerked back, looked at him and sputtered the word she had been forming— "An affair."

Her eyes widened. Other women had affairs; she didn't.

Duncan followed her out of the shower and into the bedroom, where she quickly found a discarded shirt and buttoned herself firmly into it. She'd never had an affair and Duncan was perfect affair material. "I think I'll see what's to eat," she said over her shoulder to the naked, glowering man standing in the center of the room.

"Now, get this straight...." He walked slowly toward her, all angles and smoothly moving muscles.

"Yesss?" She glanced meaningfully down his body and began to grin. He didn't bother to rephrase. He loomed over her, a tall, dangerous cowboy locked on to his prize. Then he bent, wrapped his arms around her and lifted her face to his lips. Her toes dangled above the floor. "Run that part about an affair by me again."

"You and me...and an affair. I've never had one in my entire lifetime."

"So what?" Duncan clearly lacked understanding. "Neither have I."

He'd shocked her. She'd been convinced by the way he'd kissed her, from the way he'd controlled his body, that he was very experienced. It was her turn to blink and reassemble.

Duncan leaned against the kitchen wall and watched Sybil. Dressed in his worn chambray shirt, she explored his shelves and refrigerator. The sight of her rounded, bare backside appeared each time she bent. At four o'clock in the morning, he would have preferred another enchanting session with a woman who had given every proof that she was committed to him.

"I love you.... Oh, Duncan, I love you so much...." The words were too clean, too new and fragile, riveting him.

He'd let her have her way, to his delight and fascination, and the payoff—her commitment—would be coming shortly.

She punched the buttons on his telephone. "I'd better check my messages."

As she listened, she turned away from him and her hand flattened against the wall. Her fingers trembled before she spread them on the wall and the set of her body tightened momentarily.

"Problems?" Duncan asked when she turned back, her expression taut.

She hurried to the stove and poured beaten eggs over sautéed green peppers, mushrooms and tomatoes. "Mrs. Portway. She's determined I know something about her Spanish ancestry."

He studied her as she passed, carrying omelets. Her grim expression didn't fit the easy way she could handle difficult clients. Something else bothered her. As a solitary man, Duncan recognized her privacy, and hoped that if she needed him, she would ask.

The portions on his plate wouldn't keep a bird alive, but he appreciated her efforts and the dessert that would follow.

The point was—he had her where he wanted her. With him. In his house and in his bed. He'd just let her keep pouncing and then he'd close the gate. It was just a matter of time before she said, "I do."

Marriage. The stark enormity of what he wanted with Sybil shocked him. He'd tried and failed once. They came from different worlds. Tallchiefs did not make easy relationships and were said to have backbones of steel. Sybil was too cool, too classy. Duncan settled back against the counter, tracking her movements. If she thought an affair would pacify what lay between them—

She whisked by again and he followed her over to the refrigerator and held the glasses while she poured orange juice. He was pushing the matter, but— "Earlier...when you vamped me the first time, what was that you said about fertility?"

She put the orange-juice carton back in the refrigerator and closed the door. She brushed by him and began buttering the toast, which had just popped up. She slathered on layers of butter. "Oh, you know. Emily was conceived my first time. And you...you were very with the project. Engrossed and looking like a fearless warrior. Shockingly so. You were very primitive...and sweet later. I watched you."

"I know." Duncan placed the glasses on the table and approached her. They had cried out together, their voices blending as their bodies had. He wondered if she knew how they had gripped the cradle together. That in the fiery storm of his passion, he'd heard *The woman who brings the cradle to a man of Fearghus blood will fill it with his babies....*" The idea that they could have created a life poured through him like sunlight.

He decided to be cautious about the matter. The decision was hers for now, yet he had to know. "Would it terrify you? To carry my child, I mean?"

"I was terrified once.... No, not now." She considered the idea, staring at the picture of the five Tallchiefs as children. They were black-haired demons, every one. Duncan had little doubt that his offspring would be civilized. He turned over the idea, warming to it.

He gathered his fear tight against him. Another woman had not wanted his "brats."

Sybil handed him a slice of toast and he bit into it firmly. She watched him chew and her eyes widened. She clutched the butter knife and pushed it through the butter and over to bump the plate of toast. It skidded across the counter; he caught it before it fell. "What's wrong?"

He was missing something. Sybil, tousled by passion, by his lovemaking, was showing signs of retreating. "You're not wearing a shirt," she noted, looking down to his jeans.

"You're wearing it," he reminded her, and wondered where her mind was leaping to now. His was locked on the rumpled bed upstairs.

"This has all the markings of an affair, don't you think?" Her tone was a bit too cheerful. "I mean, here we are having a snack and I'm wearing your shirt and you're only wearing jeans and well...here we are, right in the middle of an affair."

While she might like the idea of an affair, it wasn't on his menu. "No. We're talking long-term plans here. People move in and out of affairs."

Her answer didn't please him. "I haven't. You haven't. Some of them last for years. We've generally been very careful—except with each other, this time. The question is, will a relationship work between us?"

Duncan knew he was skidding on new, unbroken and foreign territory of the female mind. He decided he'd better track her thoughts carefully. She took the remainder of his toast and scooped jam onto it. She studied the blackberry gob on her fingertip for longer than made him comfortable. Then she raised it to his mouth.

Duncan sucked the sweet blob from her finger; he sensed warily that he was performing exactly to her specifications. The hair on his nape stood up, as it did in dangerous situations.

"Mmm." Her tone considered something too abstract for him to center on.

Women were shifting elements he decided, not allowing her distance from him. He liked her on his lap while they ate. She seemed to enjoy feeding him.

On the other hand, he relished placing food in her mouth. When her lips closed around his finger and sucked, Duncan lifted her in his arms and ran up the stairs.

Before dawn, Duncan shattered twice more, only to be collected by the woman holding him. This time they had rolled to the floor in a tangle of blankets and passion. They snuggled together and the smirk on Sybil's face caused him to smile. "Amazing. Who would believe your resources ran to...? I believe I just raided your resources twice in short order."

Duncan found her breast and treasured the softness lazily. He ran his thumb across the tender tip and smiled when it hardened. "Counting coup. You've been listening to Elspeth's stories of our younger days."

"Aye. Let's rest and go for three."

Mist layered Tallchief Lake and spread upon the fields below Duncan's home. On the porch, Duncan stood behind Sybil, holding her in his arms. She wore nothing but the Tallchief plaid and a mysterious smile that pleased him. He nuzzled her hair, filling his senses with the scent of her, the feel of the woman who had completed him. With the dawn, their time had come to an end and peace lay between them.

"Duncan?" She turned to lift her face for his kiss and a drift of warm strands slid silkily across his chest.

"Mmm?" He could float into eternity, holding her quietly like this. . . .

"You have to understand about Gavin. He's always protected me."

The man had come from Sybil's past and Duncan resented him. Gavin had the look of expensive breeding and manners, everything that a woman like Sybil should have. He could feel the past tugging at her, pulling her away from him, and he admitted his fear. "What is he to you? Now?"

She turned to hold him, snuggling beneath his chin. "He's my friend."

Duncan snorted, something he seemed to do more since Sybil had entered his life.

"Gavin has always felt guilty about me. His elder brother used him to lure me that night. He couldn't stop them and wanted to testify. His family wouldn't let him. When he could, he left them and has always helped me. Though relations between my family and me are strained, I care about them. Gavin votes my proxy at the family board meetings and lets me know the little things. How they look, if they talk about Emily at all—they don't.... So I guess—"

"You're friends," Duncan finished, and thanked the man who had sheltered Sybil. There, in the quiet morning with the mist enfolding them, Duncan asked again, "What promise to you haven't I kept?"

Sybil's fingers walked up his bare chest to his lips. "You said you'd dance with me. You haven't."

"I'm out of practice. I wanted to hold you in my arms—"

"You are now, aren't you? Holding me?"

He lifted her in his arms, filled with the beauty of the night past and the morning around them. She wrapped her arms around his neck, hands stroking his hair, as he began to waltz with her.

"Mmm. I knew you'd choose something old-fashioned and elegant," she murmured against his throat.

"Stay with me today." *Stay with me forever.*

"I can't. There's Emily."

Duncan hoarded other words to him as he waltzed, carrying her. *"Oh, Duncan, I love you so much."*

Nine

In the third week of August, Birk went to Arizona to post jail bond for Fiona. Then Calum and Duncan went to bail *two* Tallchiefs from the sheriff's keeping. During that visit, certain developers found that their underhanded crimes had "accidentally" surfaced.

Upon Birk's return to Amen Flats, Lacey promptly dumped a bucket of ice cubes over his head. Her work done in Arizona, Fiona headed for Montana on another environmental issue.

Wyonna grew stronger every day and had begun taking home education courses on the shelter's computer. She attended a seminar for women reshaping their lives and another one for administrating shelters. She changed her name, as though washing Jack away from her.

Duncan invited Emily and Sybil to his home for dinner and homemade ice cream. He surprised Sybil with a seafood pasta salad, served with sourdough rolls and fresh country butter. They watched the latest horror thriller, with Emily sprawled on the floor. Seated beside Sybil on the floor, Duncan ran his arm along her back. He tugged her back to rest against the couch, and other than playing with the tendrils at her nape and toying with her ear, he was very proper.

Lacey was right—Duncan's eyes were very expressive. In them, Sybil saw heat and storms and softer emotions that pulled at her heart. When his eyes drifted lazily down toward her breasts, she trembled.

Duncan took her hand just as the screen's vampire nipped a neck. He eased his fingers through hers, studying her pale, slender ones against his broader, tanned hands. Then slowly, so slowly, he raised her hand to his lips and kissed it.

Riveted to the television, Emily screamed, and Sybil's heart began beating again.

Duncan took them for walks on the mountain, pointing out a bear's cave, and deer in the meadows.

He was very courteous.

Too courteous. Sybil wanted to grab him and—

Just looking at him, especially his long, tanned body javelling into the lake, she wanted to taste what had begun. For the first time in her life, Sybil wondered if men could be flirts and teases. It was a new, disturbing thought that darkened when she was certain that Duncan was withholding himself from her.

She had gone to him that first time. But pride kept her from returning. Instead, she gave each kiss her best. She wanted him and he knew it.

Duncan Tallchief was the most contrary man she'd ever met.

The fourth week of August was the local fair and the first showing of Emily's pet calf. Emily, excited by her blue ribbon, was surrounded by leggy young westerners. Birk glanced in her direction and murmured one word: *"Boys."* Duncan's and Calum's heads went up, sighting the teenage boys surrounding Emily. In unison, the Tallchief brothers vaulted over a fence.

Duncan, Birk and Calum appeared menacing as they approached the teenage boys. All hard angles and brooding expressions, the Tallchiefs leaned against the corral. To protect Emily, they looked as though they could stand until the end of time. Elspeth shook her head. "You see what I mean? I don't know how Fiona and I managed. No wonder we were driven to... Well, I'd better not say. But the three of them weren't an easy match when holding our own."

The rodeo was Sybil's first; Duncan horrified her when he rode a bull named "Killer Deluxe." Dressed in a long-sleeved, cotton shirt, a western tooled belt, and jeans and boots, Duncan never looked more western male than when he strapped on flaring leather chaps and replaced his hat. With his leather-gloved hand wrapped in the bull rope and his other hand whipping the wind, Duncan rode the spinning, bucking monster from the open gate.

Sybil saw his essence then—grim, determined to win, all tough edges and whipcord power. The warrior within him terrified her.

She'd said she loved him. Unused to the emotion, she'd told him what lay within her heart. It had burst out of her, released by the beauty Duncan had created.

What did she know about love? What did she know about keeping it safe or nurturing it? Or blending lives?

Or taming a Tallchief?

The way Duncan rode his horse to where she sat in the grandstand, the way he crossed his arms over the saddle horn and just looked at her, sent chills up her spine. The crowd had quieted, watching her and Duncan, who showed no sign of moving. With the snow-capped mountains behind him, he appeared as enduring and hard as any western cowboy.

Next to Sybil, Elspeth sat very still, her proud profile revealing nothing. The soft curve of her lips told Sybil that Elspeth knew something no one else did, and it pleased her.

Elspeth seemed to have an unerring ability to tell just what her family would do in a certain circumstance.

Then, without warning, Duncan climbed out of his saddle, stepped across the grandstand fence and picked Sybil up in his arms. A man held his horse as Duncan settled her in his saddle and leaped up behind her. He rode around the area slowly, twice, and while she was fuming, he kissed her tenderly in front of the crowd. It was a light kiss, but a claiming one.

In the three weeks since Duncan had made love to her, Sybil could barely catch her breath. There were moments when just looking at him filled her with wonder—this strong man who could be so tender with Emily. He trembled when he kissed Sybil, devastating her and heating beneath her still-shy caresses. Yet he was too proper at times, and they hadn't made love again. Sybil ached in every fiber of her body for his love-making. His desperation had been her own.

To keep Emily from the traditional Tallchief thumb nicking and blood promise she wanted so badly, Duncan had pleaded for his abused thumb. Though Calum found an excuse, Birk had volunteered instantly. Elspeth had levied a threat against him, if he dared. It had to do with telling Lacey certain secrets. At the end of the passionate Tallchief argument, Emily agreed that she didn't need her thumb nicked. She decided to wait for a better time to argue her case.

Now, early September lit the mountains' aspens in flame colors. Mist clung in the meadows, and autumn's chill settled in the mornings. Emily had begun her first experience with public school, thrilled with wearing jeans and with nature preparing for a hard winter.

Sybil traced her finger through a square of sunshine crossing into her kitchen. She glanced at Elspeth, who was visiting for afternoon tea. She looked nothing like the woman who had shown Emily those riding tricks and warned her not to try them.

Apparently all Tallchiefs had a wild streak, Sybil decided. "You should have seen Duncan last night. We'd just gotten home from dinner and a movie and were just saying goodnight. I asked him in, but he's being very obstinate about how things look. I am not the old-fashioned one here."

She flashed an annoyed glance at Elspeth. "How things look. That's a laugh. Do you know how embarrassed I was when he just plucked me up and put me on his horse?"

"I seem to remember Mother complaining about the same thing with Dad," Elspeth murmured with a light smile.

"Well, anyway. Last night, there Duncan stood—wearing a scowl, with his hair all tousled, the way it is when he's been running his fingers through it. It's getting long, Elspeth. You should cut it."

"Me?" Elspeth's haughty tone said that she was no longer responsible for Duncan's haircuts.

"You. The barber is afraid of Duncan and you know it. I heard that once, he picked Joe up and hung him against the wall. He seems to like picking people up—" Sybil paused, thinking how magnificent Duncan looked with longer hair. It gleamed with blue-black highlights and felt so wonderfully crisp beneath her fingertips. Last night, she'd tried desperately to sleep, recognizing that she needed her rest for the morning's enormous new account. But wanting Duncan in her bed had interfered.

Dreams of him standing tall and naked—except for a small loincloth—all tanned and gleaming and powerful . . . allowed for little sleep. Add to the backdrop of rugged mountains a huge tepee and an infant in the cradleboard he held, and the dreams would destroy any woman. Sometimes she saw a baby with straight, black hair sleeping in the Tallchief cradle—

Sometimes she dreamed of Duncan moving over her, his features taut and dark and desperate, his gray eyes tinted like shifting smoke in the night sky. He treated her so carefully, entering, filling her until he seemed to touch her heart.

Oh, Duncan . . . I love you so much. . . .

Another telephone call had claimed the remainder of her peace. The man yelled obscenities at her when she blew a whistle into the phone.

The calls were sporadic and she suspected that Frank had a friend doing his dirty work. She believed he would tire of the game soon enough, and the calls seemed mild compared with those after her rape. There was an odd, ding-ding noise in the background and she'd kept tapes of the calls for legal use. Since she preferred her privacy, she'd decided against Amen Flats' law. They would just inform Duncan and she didn't want him concerned—a man who made up his own rules, he could be a disaster.

Sybil tore her flowery paper napkin in tiny shreds. Duncan was a difficult man. He could see how much she wanted him and his body gave evidence of his desire. Yet each time he set limits on his passion . . . on *her* passion. Sybil disliked his control, especially when she had locked herself to him last night. She looked at Elspeth. "You should have seen him last night. The word 'affair' came up and—"

"Don't tell me that you told Duncan that what you two have is an affair?" Elspeth lifted one black, fine eyebrow at Sybil.

"Well, I tried to. Actually, I asked when it was going to begin. . . . That I had made certain decisions and—" She glanced at Elspeth. "He seemed to grow three feet, looked horribly thunderous, his gray eyes flashing steel. I felt as if I'd stepped into the cave of some—"

"A Tallchief warrior, dear. By the way, it's true what he says about your eyes—they are the shade of topaz, and light like a tiger's when you're angry."

"Yes, well. I've been a tad disturbed by him. He can be so— I'm not ready for what Duncan wants. Whatever that is. I've been under someone or another's rule most of my life. Duncan isn't an understanding person in matters like this, Elspeth. Since I've been on my own, I've always made my decisions alone."

"Mmm." Elspeth's tone was noncommittal. She murmured, "You're about to have a visitor." ·

Duncan loomed outside the door, his horse tied to her picket fence.

Sybil glanced at Elspeth, who hadn't taken her eyes off her teacup. At times, Elspeth seemed to have the mystical powers of her shaman and seer ancestors. When Sybil opened the door, she tried a welcoming smile, which died. Looking all fierce and dressed in chaps, Duncan thrust a parcel into her hands, then bent to take her lips with a hard, hungry kiss. He lifted his head, pride flashing in his steel-gray eyes as he gazed down at her. Then, in the next instant, he was vaulting onto his saddle.

Sybil hugged the bulky parcel in one arm and covered her tender lips with her fingertips. Duncan shot one more hot look at her, then sat very straight, all broad shoulders and commanding man while his horse pranced toward Tallchief Mountain.

When Sybil finally turned, Elspeth was still sitting at her kitchen table, looking amused. Sybil managed to recover. "Oh, that man. He just swoops and claims and then he's gone."

"He'll be back. What did he bring?"

Sybil tore the wrappings away, not folding them neatly as she usually did. When she was finished, the old cradleboard lay on the table, the pale, soft doeskin gleaming in the sunshine. The rich beadwork, blue and white and red, was intricate and perfect, portraying the symbols for chief, big mountain and woman. Good omen symbols shone in the rich, buttery texture. Fringes softened the oval-shaped cradle-board, which had been strapped to the mother's back. "It's beautiful."

Elspeth traced one of the fringes and smoothed the old beads. "It was Una's," she whispered. "Tallchief's markings are on the bent wood. See the mountain?"

Feeling dazed, Sybil poured herself into her chair. "What an odd thing to give me. I was certain we had an understanding that we wouldn't exchange gifts. I have never given him anything."

"I don't think Duncan has a gift exchange on his mind. But he does set rules that suit him." Elspeth's humor lit her eyes, crinkled in the corners.

"I can't accept something that is a family heirloom." Sybil adored the cradleboard, her fingers floating over the magnificent beaded handwork and soft doeskin.

Elspeth's humor became a soft smile. "My brother is making a statement, Sybil."

Sybil stared at the gift, her eyes rounding at Elspeth's implication. "No. He's desperate *not* to have children. I know because he . . ."

When she had mentioned her potential fertility, Duncan had rushed to cleanse her. She flushed under Elspeth's humored study. "Well, I just know."

"Perhaps he's thinking more of a lasting bond and the cradleboard is symbolic of a union." Clearly Elspeth was amused at the whole incident. "Symbolism is part of Duncan's heritage, you know. He listens to the sounds of the earth and to the animals. He's very respectful and observes some of the old ways."

Sybil shook her head, disbelieving. "I know that he meditates and that he collects relics of his heritage."

Yet she'd seen Duncan carefully sidestep a plant or lift his head to watch a hawk soar.

Elspeth's hand covered Sybil's. "We share a heritage, but Duncan more than the rest goes more inside himself. He's reverent of the earth and is very complex. We've all inherited certain insights, the ability to image people, and he sees a definite, interesting image where you're concerned. I believe you may have nicked his pride, dear. I really dislike informing you of this, but I fear you are in for a battle.''

''Whatever for?''

''You'll see. He's started to grow ferns. They are responding nicely.''

Sybil shook her head. ''Ferns are strange plants for Duncan to grow.''

''Yes. He usually collects herbs from the wild. This time, the image is different, I think. You're very exotic, especially when you're fighting with him. Your coloring changes into brilliant hues, too vibrant for a mountain cat, which blends with earth tones. At first, I thought a woman of fire. But you are too sleek and graceful.'' Elspeth sipped her tea and smoothed the doeskin. ''Mmm,'' she murmured again. ''So his time has come.''

The next evening, Duncan ripped his leather gloves away. The dying light caressed Amen Flats, the shadows of the mountain swallowing it. He needed to repair fences and store more hay in the barn before he thought about the woman who rode his thoughts. He patted his horse. This time he'd chosen a calico—or pinto—that had probably descended from his father's people. Tradition was as much a part of his life as the wind or Tallchief Mountain. Or the flame-haired woman tormenting him.

He plucked a delicately laced frond away from his fringed leather jacket. Ferns liked cool, shady places away from strong winds and heat. They had to be handled gently and responded to exact watering, a gentle misting.

She wanted games. An affair. A quick hunger of bodies that offered no commitment.

His pride nicked, he would leave no room for her to do other than to make a choice.

He'd chosen the way of tradition, bringing gifts to her in a time-honored way, riding a horse that was his alone. Duncan lifted his head to the evening, inhaling the town aromas of cooking evening meals. His truck would have been faster, but he'd wanted time to think, to listen to what was in his heart. He focused on Sybil's house; she was working at her computer, her office window framing her head and shoulders. Emily was probably watching television and trying to do her homework.

Sybil was a part of his mind and his body. He did not take that lightly, nor did he accept the fences she constantly erected between them. Cool, exactly placed fences that reminded him he had no claim on her.

But he did. When his heart beat for the sight of her, when a lift of her chin set his pulse pounding, when the sound of her voice soothed the restless pacing of the wolf within him, he knew she was his other half.

Whatever lay between Sybil and him, it had brought to life primitive instincts and passions he had not experienced.

The calico nickered as Duncan slid from the saddle. He'd expected the cradleboard to be returned. Perhaps it still would be when Sybil recognized his intentions. Maybe she hadn't had time to deal with it, her work taking priority over their relationship. He would expect that. She understood priorities necessary for survival the way few people did. He honored her thinking and counted each heartbeat that the cradleboard was not returned.

He longed for her. For the sound of her voice . . . the graceful movements of her hands like fluttering doves.

Duncan's tall body tensed. He'd fought the driving urge to have her. The entering of her body was symbolic, a treasuring of her as his heart. He would not cheapen either one of them.

She cared. But she fought what was within her, what the past had caused.

Or perhaps she wanted a man like Gavin James, one with city clothing and soft ways. One who knew the right things to say and when.

Duncan glanced at the tire swing he'd made for Emily. The girl had never had a simple swing hung on a tree and she'd cried. She'd never fished in a stream or been taught to treasure nature in the wild. At thirteen, she looked how Sybil must have looked, all coltish and promising. Emily possessed a sense of humor and Duncan mourned for Sybil, who would speak little of her life. He sensed it was too dark and cold for her to share.

This time when she came to the door he handed her the string of fat fish from Tallchief Lake. The light behind her lit the fire in her loosened hair and outlined her body within the long lounging gown.

Though stunned, she held the fish firmly—his gift to her—and stood on tiptoe to receive his kiss, and his heart leaped. The kiss was so soft, the brushing of his lips on hers, her scent enfolding him. The restlessness within him quieted, eased by this woman who was part of him and yet apart.

He heard the ring the second time and realized that Emily, engrossed in the lively, loud teen show, might not answer the telephone. Sybil, her eyes shaded with dark-gold tints, continued to look at him and reached for the wall phone next to her. As the caller, a woman with a sharp voice spoke, Sybil's eyes darkened.

Duncan watched her draw within herself, close the cool, tight fronds protectively around her. The woman's knifelike voice met Sybil's cool murmurs, as though she were waiting for a quick slash.

He took the fish from her and placed them in the sink. Sybil frowned at him, listening to the caller. He sensed that her mood had changed, that all the fences were in place. That she needed his protection. Yet the look she shot him was not welcoming, and he waited, understanding that this was a battle she needed to fight alone.

"No, I am not having a tawdry affair. I am not shaming the White name again. Duncan Tallchief is not to be investigated further. Yes, I did spend the night with him. I swear, Mother, if you interfere one more time with my life, I will make no promises about the shares that Grandmother left me. Furthermore, Mother...and Father—I hear you on the extension—I am not in your keeping any longer."

Her face flushed, she gripped the telephone with fingers that were white with tension.

Duncan watched her struggle, a tangled battle of frustration, love and anger. He waited until she'd hung up the phone, tears glittering on her lashes. She leaned heavily against the wall and closed her eyes.

He wanted to go to her, hold her, but saw that now she struggled with the past. A strong woman, Sybil preferred to fight alone. He hoped that one day she would lean against him. He made a movement to leave, and her topaz eyes, glittering with tears, opened. "My mother. She's worried that I've become involved. Not that she's ever cared."

He touched her cheek, rubbed away a tear with his thumb. "You love them."

It was enough that she placed her cheek against his palm, in his keeping. "The strange thing is, I believe they love me and simply have no idea how to show it. At first they were injured by the gossip—when Emily was born. Then the breach widened. They've never been demonstrative . . . but oh, Duncan. My mother sounds so old, so worried."

"Could it be that she knows? That now you are the strong one and she knows she has failed?"

Sybil shivered and stepped back, away from his keeping. "I don't know. Sometimes I see her or Father looking at Emily and—" She shook her head. "I don't know."

"She looks like you."

"Yes." Sybil's tender tone held pride.

In another minute, he would ask if she liked his gift, the cradleboard. He would ask her if she loved him. . . .

A man of pride, Duncan moved away and into the evening shadows and the wind that told of winter's coming.

Two days later, Sybil smoothed the blue beaded mountain symbol on the doeskin moccasins. Another gift from Duncan, they had fitted perfectly, beautifully decorated in fringes and beads. When she tried them on with shaking hands, they clung to her ankles and calves.

His gifts were priceless heirlooms and she should return them. But they were a part of him and she found herself holding them close when she slept. She had to find something to give him in return . . . or force herself to return the gifts. She squared her shoulders and knew that Duncan would not be pleased. He was a man of pride . . . her pride was no small matter, pasting her together when her world had crumbled.

She leaned closer to the mirror, inspecting her eyes. Dark-gold circles with a touch of flames stared back at her. "Topaz. Tiger eyes."

She felt like a tiger now, protecting her child and her home.

Dressed in a black business suit, with her hair neatly tamed, she turned to the mirror. While Duncan's gifts moved something deep and womanly within her, the obscene calls had to be stopped. Emily had almost answered the telephone last night. Sybil firmed her mouth and picked up the bag she had packed with copies of cassettes.

Fifteen minutes later, she parked her car near the filling station. She listened carefully as the cars ran over the rubber strip, signaling the attendant. Ding-ding. Ding-ding.

The sound was the same as the background noise in the tapes. She found Jack Smith immediately, hovering around the snack and drink machines with his buddies.

"Well, lookee who's here, boys." He leered at her. "Duncan Tallchief's little woman."

Sybil contained the fury within her and continued looking at him. He shifted restlessly, his leer dying. She was so glad that Wyonna had gone through with the divorce. Wyonna had not believed Jack's promises of reform. "Jack," Sybil said coolly, "I think you might be interested in these tapes. If you call my home one more time—or any of your friends do—or if you contact me in any way, I am turning the originals over to the police."

Jack's curse broiled the room. Sybil let him run out of breath, then she nodded and walked away.

She was just making tea, when Duncan entered her house. She knew that no amount of tea would calm the emotions he could fire within her. This time there was no polite rap on her door; sweeping into her home, dressed in chaps, he was like a full-blown mountain storm filled with lightning and thunder.

"You."

The flat, deep word was an accusation that raised the hair on her body. A gunfighter's expression would be more kindly. Elspeth had been right: Duncan was a warrior. But Sybil's control was running low. Facing Jack and his buddies had trimmed away a good measure. She needed every dram of control to deal with Duncan on any level.

She wrapped the teapot in a dish towel so the tea could steep, and lifted an eyebrow to him. "Yes?"

Then, because she wanted to waylay the war brewing between them, for whatever cause, she tossed him a diversion. "I hear you're growing ferns. That must be very relaxing. A tranquil—"

"You." Duncan's gloved hand shot out to clasp the back of her neck and draw her closer. His steely gaze cut at her, damning her. "With you around, I need all the tranquillity I can manage. What the hell do you mean by facing Jack Smith—and his so-called friends—alone?" he demanded in a too-soft voice.

"I prefer to deal with unpleasantries in my own way."

"Unpleasantries? They could have raped you right there."

She drew her head back from his gloved hand. "They wouldn't. Now, let me go."

He ripped off his glove and placed his fingers on her nape. His hands trembled as he caressed her and scowled at her. "Am I hurting you?"

"No. I just don't like being manhandled and you know it."

Duncan's eyes flickered and he slowly released her. "I know." He breathed deeply, the aroma of pine and leather enfolding her. "You make your choices about what affects your life. And how you will deal with them."

She found Duncan's dark, male scent and fought longing for him. "I had a problem. I took care of it in the quietest, most efficient way I know."

"Problem? So Jack has been making obscene calls to you for how long?"

"I've had them before and much worse." Her fingers shook as she unwrapped the teapot and poured the liquid into a fragile cup. With Duncan in a mood, she felt as delicate as the china.

On the other hand, who— "Just who do you think you are to talk to me like this?" she asked, her control slipping.

Pain ripped through his eyes, darkening them before he shielded his emotions. He spoke in a whisper.

"I'm someone you should have turned to."

She'd hurt him. Duncan the defender was used to taking people under his wing. She preferred to deal with the matter by herself. The Tallchiefs could be a high-tempered, avenging clan and she liked quiet and harmony. "Duncan . . . I . . . I am used to handling my situations by myself. This doesn't involve you."

He looked down at her, his eyes flashing steel. "Think again."

She tried to rally her thoughts, to reason with him. "Duncan, we each have pasts. You struggle with pain that you haven't told anyone about."

"Such as?" He was all hunter now, not allowing her any room. He folded his arms over his broad chest and stood, legs locked apart, watching her.

She caught the bruises on his knuckles, and touched them. The way he gazed down at her was as chilly as the bottom of Tallchief Lake. "Duncan. You didn't," she managed, studying him. "I don't want any brawls because of me. I detest fighting."

"It wasn't a fight, more like a lesson." His silence accused her. Then he said too carefully, "You told me you love me. Is it true?"

Facing Duncan Tallchief was far more difficult than facing Jack Smith. "You ... I ... we.... I believe we have a ... a relationship of sorts. Neither one of us has seen anyone else—"

She found no comfort in his harsh expression. "I really should get your gifts and return them to you. They are much too priceless to give to—"

He snorted at that, looking all tall and western in his hat and boots.

The snort set her off. She saw his nostrils flare with it and his mouth tighten into a hard line. "*I* am trying here, Duncan."

"Cut my hair."

Like a flaming arrow, the order sliced into the space between them.

"What?"

"Elspeth won't do it anymore." The light caught Duncan's blue-black hair, touched his eyebrows and lashes and gleamed on his high cheekbones. Set in the shadows, his smoky gaze locked on to her.

Stunned, she took a step backward. Duncan remained as formidable as Tallchief Mountain. "I have no idea how to trim a man's hair. That isn't the topic here."

"I know. You're trying to remind me that I have no claim on you. You're trying to 'make nice,' and place everything in its righteous, cool corner. Sex, of course, is a different matter." The words cut at her.

He was too big and too dangerous to place in any corner, she thought instantly, desperately fighting to control her temper. "Duncan, I think we should both cool down—"

"Cool down? Just like that?" His mouth took hers, his arms wrapping her tightly against him. The heavy, rapid thudding of his heart hit her palm like a hammer. Her toes left the floor as his lips burned hers.

His need for her was too raw, his body thrusting against her. But she wasn't afraid—this was Duncan...Duncan...the word became a litany, raw with emotion and physical need to have him fill her, and only him. She buried her hands in his hair, his hat tumbling to the floor. Duncan eased her to the counter and moved between her legs.

His hand tugged at her jacket and found her breast, claiming it. His other hand found her bottom, opening to cup her tightly.

This was Duncan, elemental, passionate, meeting her desire and claiming her—

She cried out, needing him, her body weeping for his...her legs caught his hips, bringing him so close...so close and powerful.

Then he was shaking, burying his face in her shoulder and dragging in huge, unsteady breaths against her skin. He rocked her in his arms for one beat of her pulse. Then he moved abruptly away, as though tearing himself away from his very heart.

His thumb moved across her swollen, tender lips. The smoky tint of his eyes darkened; his expression slid to regret.

And then he was gone.

Ten

Duncan parked the rental car on the Whites' Seattle-mansion driveway. Rain slashed at the car, but the storm was no more elemental than what had driven him here—the need to see Sybil, to hold her. The lit entryway behind the pristine pillars was barely visible in the heavy downpour.

"Oh, Duncan . . . I love you so much. . . ."

He gripped the steering wheel with his gloved hands. He was too used to his own rules. He should have called Sybil before he left to find the boy. The ten-year-old had become lost on a camping trip. He'd survived in a protected mountain cave until Duncan had found him. The boy was savvy once he'd discovered he was lost. His Boy Scout survival skills had kept him alive in severe weather.

While Duncan was in the area, he'd helped in a manhunt in the mountains. The killer was also skilled at survival and dangerous.

Duncan drew a steadying breath into his lungs. He hadn't slept in how long? Not on the flight from Denver. In the six days since he'd seen Sybil, Duncan realized that he'd had only minutes of sleep. Six long, hard days ago—that was the last time Duncan saw Sybil.

The Tallchiefs weren't an easy family to understand; their emotions ran deep. With the lack of sleep and his frustration, Duncan knew his usually calm nerves were stretched like bowstrings.

When Duncan thought of Sybil coolly entering Jack Smith's hangout, a place with a back room— He heard a crack and forced his fingers to release the steering wheel.

When he had called Elspeth earlier that evening, she'd told him that Sybil had left two days ago. Emily was attending school, staying with Elspeth.

He'd tried his message machine, praying that Sybil's voice would be on it, and it was. "Duncan, I'm leaving now. Don't try to contact me—" Static had blocked out her words and then, "I can't go on like this . . ." More static. "Our relationship has never been good—" Another message overlaid the rest.

She didn't want to see him again. A can't-be, you're-dumped message on a machine.

Duncan glanced at the streetlight, a dim glow in the sheets of rain. Sybil was probably making arrangements to return to the life she'd known.

He forced himself to breathe, and caught the scent of his last campfire. He glanced in the rearview mirror, and caught his savage scowl. He was too tired to be calm with her and shouldn't have come. He'd lost his temper and now Sybil was running from him. He couldn't leave it like that, couldn't write nice notes and leave telephone messages. He should have told her he loved her, should have said the words women needed to hear.

As Duncan walked past the butler, the man's expressionless eyes took in his battered western hat. Duncan hadn't shaven in days and his hair was past his collar. The butler's gaze slid to Duncan's flannel shirt, his worn and dirty jeans and scuffed western boots. "Sir? May I ask the nature of your visit?"

"To retrieve my wife. My name is Duncan Tallchief." Hell, he'd been retrieving everyone else— Duncan leveled a look at the butler, who backed up a step. Sybil was the other part of Duncan, and in his heart, he believed she was his wife. She should have waited. But since she hadn't, Duncan planned to—what? Capture her would be good, he decided darkly. He wasn't the kind to argue, but Sybil made him want to rant and yell.

The butler cleared his throat. "I see. And what, if I may ask, is her name?"

My heart. My own. My life. Duncan looked steadily at the man. "Sybil. I'm not in the mood for word games. Just get her."

"I see," the butler said crisply. "Very well. Wait here while I check with Mr. White—"

Duncan walked past the butler and into a well-lit, stylish room, a fire blazing in the fireplace. Dressed in slacks and a lounging jacket, a tall, gray-haired man stood slowly. A woman, an older version of Sybil, wearing an expensive sweater and slacks, came to the older man's side. "I'm calling the police."

"Do that." Duncan didn't bother to remove his hat. He watched the older couple take in his appearance—that of a dirty, tough cowboy. "But I'll have my say anyway. You're looking at your future son-in-law, and we're going to get a few things straight."

"Mr. Duncan Tallchief—" the butler started to say.

"Son-in-law?" both Whites asked incredulously, dismissing his name.

Duncan nodded. He peeled away his gloves and tucked them into his leather belt. "I'll treat her well. You're welcome to visit us. You're welcome in our home. Until you hurt either Sybil or Emily. I've come to take her back with me."

"Now, listen here you—" Mr. White began.

"Dear..." Mrs. White's voice held a plea for patience. "Ah...sit down, won't you...ah...Mr...?"

"Tallchief. Duncan Tallchief. I'll make this short and sweet. I'm not in a good mood. I'm from Wyoming. I've just run six days without anything called sleep and have tracked a killer through a mountain range." When Mrs. White gasped, Duncan softened his image. "Don't worry. I'm not wearing my gun or knife. Just get Sybil for me, will you?"

He watched the Whites trace his features, picking out the darker skin tones of his Native American ancestor. Mrs. White sat abruptly; her hand went to her throat. Duncan was in no mood to be sympathetic. These people had wounded Sybil and left Emily unloved. "Are you going to get Sybil? Or do I do it myself?"

"So you're the one who has ruined her. I suppose Sybil should deal with the mess she has created this time." Mr. White waved the hovering butler to the task.

"Ruined her?" Duncan asked very carefully, as he sprawled in a chair. He draped one leg over the arm. If the inference was that Sybil was a loose woman— "It's been a long day. Why don't you explain that remark?"

"She's not herself. She's overly distraught and acting strange. Rather politely argumentative," Mrs. White explained anxiously. "We've been trying to reason with her. She could need medication and a long rest. She…mmm…has had other experiences and we've had to do the same. Though this time, she seems oddly determined in a cool manner. Do you, ah, know her background?"

"I do." Duncan caught Sybil's scent and slid his eyes to see her leaning against the door frame. She was barefoot and her arms were crossed over her chest. He couldn't read her expression.

She'd expect him to act like a savage. He felt like one now. There wasn't an ounce of warmth in her parents. No wonder she preferred to keep her life streamlined and without the interference of emotional ties except for Emily.

She belonged in a mansion. Dressed in white, satin lounging pajamas, her flame-tinted hair tumbling around her shoulders, she caused his heart to stop. The ten feet between them was too far. Just seeing her settled the rage that had been burning in him. "Hello, Sybil."

"Hello, Duncan. Where are your chaps?" Her eyes drifted over him, her expression slightly amused. He hadn't bothered to do up the upper buttons of his shirt and her gaze brushed his chest, paused there, before traveling to his boots.

He wasn't amused. Every instinct told him to carry her away, back to Tallchief Mountain.

He caught the wiggling of her toes, and it reminded him of a mountain cat twitching its tail. She was enjoying his confrontation with her parents.

Mrs. White fluttered a handkerchief to her nose. "Dear. Sybil. Be reasonable. You can't possibly be . . . be enthused about this . . . this person."

"He has his moments. Now isn't one of them, apparently. He's got that brooding, dangerous hunter look on him, and I'll bet he's just gotten back from a manhunt. He's wonderful with Emily and beautiful in kilts. Wonderful legs."

"Goodness!"

Sybil lifted an eyebrow. "Didn't you get my message that I would be calling you soon?"

"The machine malfunctioned in the storm." Duncan forced himself to sit still. *"Our relationship has never been good. . . . He has his moments. . . . He's wonderful with Emily—"* Duncan clung to each word.

She might be enjoying tormenting him, but he wanted to hold her, to tell her that she was a part of him. He noted the lift of her chin and the sheltered anger of her eyes. Pride ran through her, just as it ran through him. "Did you miss me?" he asked bluntly.

"Mmm. Mildly. The last time we saw each other, you weren't exactly reasonable."

"Sybil." Duncan paused for breath, his control unsteady. "You know why, sweetheart."

"You came to defend me, didn't you? To tuck me under your wing, where nothing could hurt me."

"Is that so bad?" They were suddenly on elemental ground now, where it was too dangerous to move quickly.

"I came here to settle the past. You can't protect me from that. It happened. Our relationship—my parents and myself—has never been good."

Duncan inhaled sharply. The "relationship" she'd been talking about in her message was not with him but with her parents!

Sybil's deep-gold eyes locked with his. "Mother, Father, I want to introduce to you Duncan Tallchief. He's descended from a Scotswoman and the Sioux chieftain who captured her. Duncan has two sisters and two brothers, and each is very special. They're loyal and loving to one another. Duncan raises sheep and cattle on Tallchief Mountain. He is very good to Emily. His entire family has adopted her and she's determined to nick her thumb in a blood promise. Duncan and his brothers are her Black Knights and she is their princess."

Her expression darkened. "He wants me to cut his hair and wait on him. I've only just discovered why. He loves me. He cares so much, but he hasn't quite gotten the knack of telling me. I have high hopes for improvement. What is important for you to know is that he treasures those he loves. Treasures. He listens. He cares."

Mrs. White gave every evidence of swooning as Sybil lifted her finger and curled it, signaling Duncan to come to her. "But right now, Duncan is obviously tired and probably not sweet. Come to my room, Duncan. I'm afraid my parents can't handle any more Tallchief manners tonight."

"Your room!" Mr. White exploded. "Not in my house. You are not taking this . . . this bounty hunter to your room."

"We can go elsewhere."

Sybil's challenge cost her; Duncan saw her warring with her love of her parents and her own course. Choices of the heart weren't easy. He prayed he was on her menu, and stood.

"I'd rather talk to you in private, away from here."

"My terms, Duncan. I say here."

He glared at her and found the tigress leaping from her eyes. He took a deep, steadying breath and knew that the gamble was too big. She wanted her way—this time. It was important in the battles with her parents. He nodded curtly.

"Goodness!" Mrs. White exclaimed, taking in Duncan's height and size. "You . . . you're so big. So . . . cowboy."

Sybil's gaze ran coolly down him. She tapped her finger on her lips. "Yes. Goodness, he is, isn't he? He's also not in a good mood, from the shade of his eyes and that black scowl. He's in his gunfighter-showdown mood and not exactly reasonable. The Tallchiefs are like that, but also caring, emotional and delicate. They have to be protected at times. So I'm taking him to my room. Good night, Father. Good night, Mother. We'll see you at breakfast. Come along, Duncan."

"He's delicate?" Mr. White's yell was pure outrage as Duncan followed Sybil up the winding, elegant stairway.

Duncan tensed at the shrill cry. It boasted of a bully's ownership.

On the other hand, he didn't like Sybil's "delicate" remark, either. Perhaps he had something in common with Mr. White.

"Sybil? Sybil, dear. You should put on your robe," Mrs. White called, following them.

Duncan noted the sincere concern in the woman's voice.

Sybil turned to coolly look down at her mother.

Duncan's eyes were on a level with her breasts. She caught his hot look and flung it back at him, taking in his hat, opened shirt, dirty jeans and boots.

"Sybil, don't you dare take that man to your room. You always were a rebel and you've caused your own problems. How dare you bring your paramours here."

"If he leaves, I leave. And I won't be back. We'll talk all about this in the morning after everyone has had a good rest."

Her mother turned white. "You don't mean that. This...this cowboy is a bad influence. Just looking at the two of you, there on the stairway, your satin to his leather, anyone can see you're not a match. Dear, you have breeding and manners. He...he's a savage from Wyoming."

She seemed to wilt against the wall as Sybil just stared at her, then turned to continue up the magnificent stairway.

He forced his eyes away from Sybil's swaying backside, clad in satin. Unused to following orders, he wasn't happy that the woman he'd come to claim was issuing them.

She closed the door to the sumptuous bedroom and rounded on him, topaz eyes blazing. "Exactly what do you mean coming here? And telling Morris that I'm your wife?"

At a loss for words, frustrated and deeply tired, Duncan reacted immediately. He tugged her into his arms and found her mouth with his.

Sybil jerked her head back. "Oh, no. Not that darned Tallchief, mind-blasting kiss. I've been holding my own through the disasters of the past two days. You're not getting around this by kissing the daylights out of me."

"Fine. You can kiss them out of me." Duncan leaned down slowly to brush a kiss on one corner of her lips, then the other. "You taste like honey."

Sybil closed her eyes, leaned slightly toward him for an instant and then firmly pushed her hands flat against his chest.

"Duncan, you look like living death, and if I let you run over me now, I know I'll regret it. You've got your defender look written all over you and I won't have it. Not now."

Beneath the satin her hip was curved, full, all woman. He squeezed slightly and brushed another kiss against her cheek. Her breath caught and her hand lifted to smooth his stubble-rough cheek. There was tenderness beneath her touch and Duncan almost sighed as she stroked him and asked, "Why are you growing ferns?"

He caught her bottom lip with his teeth. She tasted like cinnamon and silk. "They remind me of you. I've been studying them. Cool. Private."

She laughed shakily. "I was cool and private. Before you."

When her fingers began unbuttoning his shirt, Duncan captured them and lifted them to his lips. "I'm dirty."

"You're always very careful to be gentle with me, aren't you? To touch me with reverence."

He rubbed his nose against hers. "Your parents are probably aghast."

She grinned at his use of the proper word and continued unbuttoning his shirt. "Yes, probably. We've been battling for two days now. They're not at all happy with me."

She pushed him toward the bathroom and, when his back was turned, patted his bottom. "Now, off you go. We'll talk later."

For a moment, Duncan stood absolutely still, his body taut. He devoured the thought that she had patted him affectionately. The way a man might pat a woman. The light gesture from her, his first, stunned him. It was no light thing when a woman like Sybil demonstrated affection. Obviously Sybil felt she had that right.

Obviously he liked it. It was an encouraging little demonstration that perhaps she wasn't tossing him out of her life.

Duncan felt the tension ease from his tense shoulders. He could deal with Sybil's feminine hand on his backside. "Do that again."

This time her touch was a caress, accompanied with a light kiss on his shoulder. "That's nice," he said, meaning it.

"Go."

Duncan bathed, then shaved with her razor. Her scents clung to the bath. Pretty, expensive Parisian oils and salts lined the luxurious tub and ferns of every kind stood beneath the huge, etched windows. He hurried and prayed that Sybil was in a gentle mood. He didn't trust the banked fire beneath her lashes. He swung open the bathroom door and stepped into the room, a towel around his hips.

Mrs. White was standing by Sybil, and her eyes widened. She glanced nervously at her daughter. "Is he safe?"

Sybil smiled, her eyes slanting with humor. "I hope not. Out, Mother. I'm going to marry this man as soon as possible. We'll talk over breakfast."

Mrs. White's diamond-studded hand gripped the door frame as Sybil began to close the door. "Dear. Dear, you know the guest room can be ready in minutes. Ah . . . wouldn't that be more comfortable?"

"No. He's tired and he needs me. He's come all this way for me. Shoo, Mother."

"Well, I . . . dear, will you be all right? We could have him forcibly ejected."

Sybil laughed outright. "I doubt it."

"But you know, dear, a wedding takes months of planning. There's the guest list—" Mrs. White's eyes grew large, as though she'd just realized there might be more Tallchiefs attending the event.

Sybil placed an arm around her mother and bent to kiss her forehead. "Don't worry, Mother. The rest of them are quite tame."

Duncan noted that Sybil was trying to comfort her mother. When hugged, the older woman had tensed, but then had settled against her daughter. Perhaps she knew it was time to change, to let the past go and adapt to the future.

When the door closed, Duncan forced himself to prowl around Sybil's room, studying it. All whites and pinks and ruffles, with a huge, canopied bed filled with more ruffles. Dolls peered from a packing box. "I want Emily to have them. My parents want them to remain in the White keeping," Sybil murmured. "It's a minor tug-of-war, but an important step forward. They've agreed that my daughter should have them."

He saw the pain moving through her before she turned to him. "You're here to carry me off, aren't you, Duncan Tallchief? You actually think that you can just—well, you can't. Not this time. You've complicated a few things, but nothing I can't deal with. You've just escalated what must be done, the meeting of terms. I love my parents, and deep down, I believe they love me. So I had planned a nice, quiet balancing of our relationship. A gentle nudge in the right direction. Then here you are, the perfect picture of a western bounty hunter."

"Are you going to marry me?" His voice sounded coarse, unsteady, raw with the emotions lashing him.

She avoided the answer he wanted to hear. "You could have waited to be invited, you know. But, then, you missed me, didn't you?" She slid his words back to him on a platter.

"Yes. Are you leaving Amen Flats?" He would move to be near her. A modern relationship tuned to air flights and schedules wouldn't do. He needed her too much.

She walked slowly, gracefully, to him and tugged the knot of the towel away. "Come to bed, Duncan. Rest. You look so tired. We'll talk in the morning."

Unused to having his schedule set for him, Duncan stood very still. "You've planned a lot of morning talk, sweetheart."

"Yes, but not now. Come here." She eased onto the cream-tinted satin sheets and waited. She crooked her finger again and blew him a kiss. "Come here, big man. I won't hurt you. Don't look like you're expecting a tiger to pounce."

"I could use that guest room. Or a motel."

"I know, you're old-fashioned. You can't go anywhere because Morris is washing your clothes. Nothing else will fit you. I just want to hold you. You look so worn. Come to me, Duncan Tallchief. I'll keep you safe."

Duncan climbed into the bed carefully. It creaked with his weight, and in the shadows he found Sybil watching him. He lay very still, his nerves raw with wanting her. To hold her, to make love to her, to show her with his body how much he loved and cherished her. Fear that he might hurt her, that his passions ran too deep for his control, stayed him.

In the shadows, a quick movement of lace and ruffles brought Sybil's satin-covered body over him.

"You are mine, Duncan Tallchief. Mine. Got it?"

He tenderly placed his hands on her waist and she smiled, bending to kiss him lightly. Her hand smoothed the hair on his chest. "So proper. Not comfortable with lying beneath my parents' roof?"

Her fingertip toyed with his nipple. "It's my house, really. Upon the event that I marry. I've been defending you for two days, Duncan, and doing a neat job of it, too. I never really cared to battle my parents over anything, anyone...except Emily. Then you show up, looking like a gunslinger out for trouble, and tomorrow I'll have to soothe them all over again. Getting my parents used to the idea that I'll be living in Wyoming and married to a Tallchief is something I had hoped to do gently. The dolls were just a minor ploy in my plans."

His throat dried instantly and his fingers tightened on her waist. His heart raced painfully.

Sybil squirmed closer. "I bought a haircutting set. I've been taking lessons."

He decided that he'd better remain quiet and let her take the lead. "You have?"

She played with his hair, trailed it over a lacy ruffle and studied the contrast. "Your heart is beating like a tom-tom. Try to relax."

"I could do that a lot easier if you'd run the marriage thing by me again," he returned unsteadily.

She laid another raven strand against the cream-and-pink lace. "Layering, I think. I hope you'll be patient my first few times...of course, I could try with someone else. Calum or Birk. Elspeth has such lovely long hair that I wouldn't dare."

"What's hair got to do with anything?" he demanded.

Sybil bent to kiss him and snuggled close, her arms around his neck as they shared the pillow. "It was important to you that I cut your hair. At first I thought it was ugh-me-male whimsy. Then I remembered how you looked when my hands touched you—that stark, waiting desperation. You like my hands on you. I believe that to you it was symbolic of a commitment from me. That I would care for you. I think, by the way, that you'll be very easy to tame," she added clinically, then bit his earlobe.

"You do, huh?" Duncan tried to think as she moved his hand to cover her breast.

"Thinking near you isn't possible. I needed distance to place everything in line. You told me with the cradleboard and with the other gifts, didn't you?"

He treasured her softness wound tight around him, the lovely curve of her breast that she had given to his care. "Yes. I found words would not come."

Her hands smoothed his cheeks, tracing a series of small cuts. He'd been too anxious to come to her. Her eyes were gentle upon him. "You've kept your fears locked to yourself for so many years that you don't know how to tell me . . . it's all right, Duncan. I know how hard it was for you and that emotions move deeply within you which I can't understand. But I know that you love me, just as I know that one day the words will come easier."

She bent to kiss him. "Last night, I dreamed I told you that, and you picked me up and ran to your tepee. There you did wonderful things with me. I was wearing a wedding band—so were you." Her lips brushed his throat.

Duncan rolled, easing her beneath him. For a moment they stared at each other in the shadows, then Duncan tugged at her elastic waistband, a gentle suggestion. "Did you like that dream?" he asked very carefully.

"Yes," she whispered, her fingers dragging through his hair and caressing his taut shoulders. "Yes."

Together they removed her clothes and Duncan settled easily upon her, viewing the picture she made. With her hair tumbling over the pale lace, her body flowing, warming to his. His eyes ran down the length of their tangled limbs, the melding of her breasts with his tanned chest. In the shadows, the tiger-woman flickered, challenging him, loving him.

He slowly bent to take her breast, to suckle her tenderly, this woman he loved. She tasted of honey and promised the future. He nipped her gently, caught the heat moving through her, the dampness of her body preparing for his.

Cautiously Duncan rested against her, fearing that he would rush, when he wanted his body to tell of his love. She bit her lip and lay beneath him like warm silk, opening, inviting him to her care. She trembled now, her hands fluttering lightly across his shoulders.

Duncan pressed his parted lips to the smooth flesh of her other breast, and found the tight bud waiting for him. She touched him, soothing his length, coaxing him within her moist folds. When he eased deeper, she closed her eyes, taking her pleasure within her. She trembled and softened and flowed beneath him, around him, yet Duncan treasured the flush riding her face, the pulse pounding in her throat. There would be other times, when he would want her quickly, fiercely. But now they were sealing the marriage that would come and he wanted to take each moment into his heart.

In the night, her eyes were tender upon him. "You fill me so completely. More than this, my gentle lover, you fill my heart."

He raised her left hand to his lips, kissing the finger that would wear his ring. "In my heart, we were married that first time."

"Yes. I think I knew it when our hands locked on the cradle."

Duncan closed his eyes, not daring to hope that she would want his child.

"I expect to make the legend come true and fill that cradle with your babies, Duncan."

Her words brought emotions so primitive they ripped through him and he could not contain them. Duncan groaned, straining to withhold his driving need to release himself within her. She gripped his arms and raised her hips, receiving him deeply. He tried to be gentle, caressing her breast, taking it to suckle deeply. All woman and power, she rippled beneath him, capturing him in a tangle of arms and legs and moist power. He was hers and she was his, and they were of one soul, one body, one heart. When she tightened her caress, straining, meeting his kiss desperately, crying out his name, Duncan felt himself tumbling, spilling, giving himself to her. He shattered on the pinnacle of their storm, heard himself crying out to her that he would love her until the stars were no more.

Gently, so gently as an autumn leaf settles to the ground, he settled upon her. Sybil claimed him gently, easing his head to rest upon her breasts. "You say such lovely things, Duncan

Tallchief," she whispered shakily against his ear, her hands stroking his back.

He had heard himself telling her things that lay within his heart, images of her as his wife, his love. That she filled his heart the way the sun fills the sky. That she was his dove, his other half, his heart. That she had made his soul take flight, and when he saw her his heart fluttered like the heart of a small rabbit sheltering in the bush. That his life lay within her hands; that dawn was no more beautiful than her.

Duncan kissed the flushed side of her throat. "They're true...." Within the warmth of her body, tangled in her care, sleep dragged him away from what he wanted to say.

During the night, she came softly to him, enfolding him. Then before dawn he awoke, fearing a dream. Sybil lay cradled beside him, fragile and pale, her hair tumbled around them. He bent over her, anxious to see if he'd hurt her in his passion, filled with the wonder of her loving him. Her lips curved slowly as he touched them, his hardened body brushing her soft hip.

When he bent to kiss her breasts, Sybil's hands and body caressed him. "Again?"

"Yes," he whispered against her soft stomach.

"Yes," she returned, receiving him like silk meant for his touch.

Epilogue

Almost one year later, Duncan lay in the tepee he had built near the lake. The early-August night was cool, animals moving in the meadows, the owls hooting. In the center of the tepee was a small fire, which lit his wife and the baby nursing at her breast.

The firelight caught the tangle of her hair, loose around her bare shoulders. His daughter's blue-black shock of hair contrasted with Sybil's glowing, ivory skin. The baby's blanket was spread across her lap—a soft Tallchief tartan woven by Elspeth. Sybil's wedding ring glowed on her finger; he wore the matching one.

This was their retreat, usually shared by Emily, who was now attending a weavers' fair with Elspeth. Sybil's daughter thrived in her new life, just as her mother did.

Sybil discovered a beautiful Tallchief tradition, that of the Bridal Tepee. Though made of modern canvas, the tepee signified that a Tallchief had claimed a true love. When Tallchief realized how deeply he loved Una, his captive bride, he had constructed a beautiful new tepee for his love. Down through the Tallchief generations, the Bridal Tepee was a statement of commitment and bonds of the heart, a home to nourish that love and shelter the family that would come.

Sybil wanted her new husband alone; he had been very, very good throughout the formal wedding that had pacified her parents. In fact, he had wooed them into a begrudging respect for the man who loved their daughter. Duncan and Sybil spoke their vows again in the tepee, and Sybil had worn the beaded doeskin shift, a Tallchief legacy for brides. She'd come to him, humbling him with promises that she would keep for a lifetime. He'd given his heart to her and his pledge, taking her gently, reverently, as though together they would put away the past. For the rest of his life, Duncan would see his bride lift away the soft shift and come to him. To their new life.

At first the Whites were stunned with the small considerations he gave them—pictures of Sybil with Emily. Pictures of Emily grinning, her hand upon the new life nestling in Sybil's body. Though their relationship was tenuous, the Whites did accept Emily, and Sybil lost her tenseness around them. In a stiff, formal way they were trying to relate.

"I love you, Mrs. Tallchief," Duncan whispered. At times he could not believe their happiness, or that their child, Megan, suckled at her breast.

"I know, and I love you," Sybil replied, the dark gold of her eyes catching the firelight.

In the flickering light, the old cradle seemed to glow, waiting for the baby—

The woman who brings the cradle to a man of Fearghus blood will fill it with his babies. . . .

Duncan met his wife's mysterious, sultry look. When the baby lay safely in the cradle, she would come to him. Then he added his thoughts to the legend—*and she would capture his heart.*

* * * * *

Legends of the Tallchiefs

Tallchief and Una Fearghus
(A Sioux Chieftain captures a Scots bondwoman who tames him.) 5 children.

Liam and Elizabeth Tallchief
(As a virgin, the English lady would inherit an empire; to save her sister from torture, she takes an unwilling staked-out half-breed. Out for revenge, he finds love.) 3 children.

Jake and LaBelle Tallchief
(This lady jewel thief and matador wants no part of the dirt-poor, hardened rancher with adopted, untamed sons. He turns up at her fancy soiree and blackmails her into marriage.) 2 children.

Matthew and Pauline Tallchief
(Amen Flats has never been big enough for them since they were children. As bodyguard to the threatened lady judge, tough tracker Matthew stakes his bridal claim with Greek mythology.) 5 children.

Duncan m. Sybil   Calum   Birk   Elspeth   Fiona
    |
   Emily
Megan

Duncan—The woman who brings the cradle to a man of Fearghus blood will fill it with his babies.

COMING NEXT MONTH